How Do You Lose Those Ninth Grade Blues?

ALSO BY BARTHE DE CLEMENTS

Nothing's Fair in Fifth Grade

How Do You Lose Those Ninth Grade Blues?

a novel by
BARTHE DE CLEMENTS

The Viking Press, New York

This book is dedicated to my children, Nicole, Mari, Christopher, and Roger.

First Edition
Copyright © 1983 by Barthe DeClements
All rights reserved
First published in 1983 by The Viking Press
40 West 23rd Street, New York, New York 10010
Published simultaneously in Canada by Penguin Books Canada Limited
Printed in U.S.A.
1   2   3   4   5   87   86   85   84   83

Library of Congress Cataloging in Publication Data
DeClements, Barthe.   How do you lose those ninth grade blues?
Summary: Though no longer a fat girl, Elsie, now fifteen,
still has trouble believing anyone could love her, and that
old fear threatens her relationship with her boyfriend.
[1. Obesity—Psychological aspects—Fiction] I. Title.
PZ7.D3584Ho   1983   [Fic]   83-5750   ISBN 0-670-38122-5

Words from the choral edition of "Amazing Grace," adapted and
arranged by John Coates, Jr., copyright © 1971 by
Shawnee Press, Inc. Used by courtesy of Shawnee Press, Inc.

Contents

Scoping Out the Frosh

I checked my school map at the door of the commons. If I went straight through and out to the courtyard, I should be facing the building with the home ec rooms. I put my map in my Pee Chee so I wouldn't look like a freshman, and I'd started weaving my way past the crowd around the Coke machines when someone yelled.

"Hey, Fatty!"

That wasn't me any more, so I kept on walkin'.

"Hey-ey, Elsie!"

I turned to see Jack lounging against the benches. "Hey-ey, *Red!*" I said back, and walked toward him. "I didn't recognize you. You grew another foot this summer."

"Lucky you didn't shrink again."

1

"Shrink?" the boy beside Jack said.

"This is Craddoc," Jack told me.

Craddoc looked down at me with one eyebrow raised. "You've been shrinking?"

"When I first met Jack in fifth grade, I was four by four," I explained.

Jack nodded. "Bubble gut to fox in four easy years."

A bell rang and I stepped back a bit. "I better go."

"Relax," Jack said. "Nobody expects you to find your class on time the first day."

Being late made me nervous. Craddoc noticed. "Which way you headed?"

"To home ec. I think it's that way." I pointed to the double doors on the west side of the commons.

"Where's your locator card?"

I pulled the card out of my purse and handed it to him as we walked through the doors and out to the courtyard.

"Home ec, English, concert choir, geometry . . ." Craddoc read. "Geometry? You took algebra in eighth grade?"

"Math's easy for me."

"I guess."

He steered me down the corridors, and kids called out to him.

"How you doing, Craddoc?"

"You going to make state this year?"

I tried to dredge up something else for us to talk about. Craddoc wasn't one of Jack's usual rowdy friends. Finally

2

I came up with, "How long have you known Jack?"

"All my life. Our mothers are old friends, and the families get together about once a month. I always thought of Jack as Kevin's wild younger brother, and now he's in high school." He stopped at the home ec door. "You just know Jack at school?"

"Uh . . . mostly. And a few parties."

"Hmmm. Well, see you later, Elsie."

Jenny was sitting at one of the tables in the room, and I sat down beside her.

"Who was that cute guy?" she asked.

"Craddoc somebody. He's a friend of Jack's."

"Students!" the home ec teacher said. "Quiet down so I can call your names."

The teacher called my name, Elsie Edwards, and Jenny's name, Jenifer Sawyer. The only other name I recognized was Sharon Hinkler. I caught a glimpse of her across the room, and I could see she still had the stupid pink barrette in her hair that she'd worn in grade school.

The teacher passed out a ditto of a two-week unit. I picked mine off the table and had begun reading about keeping food preparation areas clean when Jenny whispered, "Come over after school, O.K.?"

"O.K.," I whispered back.

Jack was in my second period English class, but nobody I knew was in concert choir. The teacher was flapping around, pulling out music folders from a box on the piano, so I waited by the choir room door with some of the other freshmen. After he had two tall stacks on the piano bench, he noticed us.

"Come on in. Come on in. Don't just stand there. Sopranos here, altos here, tenors here, and basses here." He fluttered his hands in the direction of the steps in front of him, and we found our places among the returning students.

"Now. Where are the roll sheets?" The teacher looked wildly through his junk on the podium until a tall, zit-faced boy in the baritone section bounded down the steps to pick the folded sheets out of the teacher's jacket pocket and hand them to him.

The teacher laughed and rolled his eyes toward the ceiling. I decided I was going to like him.

"I'm Mr. Krakowski," he said. "Now, let's see who you are."

Mr. Krakowski called the roll by hitting a note on the piano and asking each student in turn to sing the scales. He started with the soprano section. I licked my lips and smiled to myself in anticipation. Ethel, the small girl standing next to me, wasn't smiling. Mr. Krakowski hit a C for her, and her face went beet-red by the end of the last "la."

He played an A for me. When I finished, he stared at me thoughtfully with his fingers curled against his mouth. "Let's try another one, Elsie." This time he struck a C. I opened my mouth wide again and sailed up and down the scales, holding the last "la" for an extra beat.

4

"Hmmm." Mr. Krakowski scribbled something on his roll sheet and went on to Leah, the girl on the other side of me. She was smiling, too. And with good reason. When all fifty students had sung the scales, Mr. Krakowski put on a record and told us to pay attention. The song was "Amazing Grace." Aw right! That had been one of Mrs. Morrison's favorites in junior high.

The piano player passed out the music folders before she sat down on the bench. As I leafed through the music to find the spiritual, I noticed "Fircrest High School, Edmonds, Washington" was stamped on each page. Mr. Krakowski tapped his baton on his music stand before half the kids had found their places. "Come on. You're wasting our time. Come on." After the rustle had subsided, he gave us further instructions.

A soprano was to sing the first verse, the altos were to join in on the second, and the whole choir was to sing the third and fourth verses. The first order of business, therefore, was to choose the soprano. Mr. Krakowski would pick the top three contenders, with the class voting on the final soloist.

"If you don't want to try out for a solo, don't sing," he said. The way Ethel slunk back, I knew she wouldn't; the way Leah lifted her chest, I knew she would.

"Otherwise," he went on, "keep singing until I touch you or point to you."

Mr. Krakowski's baton went up, he nodded to the piano player, his baton swooped down, and we began, "Amazing

5

grace! how sweet the sound, That saved a wretch like me! I once was lost . . ." Mr. Krakowski moved through the soprano section, leaning his head down to hear our individual voices. I heard him say, "Sh!" to a few singers, and out of the corner of my eye saw him poke a few more. The third time through the song, there were three of us left, Leah and I and a black-haired girl with glasses named Imogene.

Imogene was the first to try out. She clutched her music in her fists and huddled close to the piano, looking like she wanted to crawl inside of it.

"Stand up tall," Mr. Krakowski ordered. "If you can't sing in front of the class, how can you sing in front of an audience?"

Imogene had a pretty voice, what we could hear of it, but she obviously hadn't been taught "impact" by Mrs. Morrison. There was no problem hearing Leah. When she finished, some of her friends clapped for her, which caught Mr. Krakowski's frown.

Then my turn. I started softly, "Amazing grace! how sweet the sound," gradually let my voice out on "Was blind, but now I see," and belted "And grace will lead me home." I finished to total silence.

"Umm . . . uh . . . you three girls wait outside while the class takes a vote." Mr. Krakowski waved us to the door.

On the way out Leah looked back at her friends, pointed to her chest, and mouthed, "Me, me, me."

6

When we were called back in, Mr. Krakowski held my arm while he let the other two girls take their places on the stands. "Well, Elsie"—he smiled down at me—"I guess you're our first soloist."

At the bell I floated out of the choir room with little Ethel at my heels. "You sure sing good," she said before she left me in the hall.

I had to think a minute. Which class was next? Geometry? Geometry, room 36. Right. I bumped into the back of a letter jacket as I burrowed my way down the hall. I let the crowd surge ahead of me so the boy wouldn't know who had hit him when he looked around. At least he wasn't Craddoc.

I had lunch with Jenny, and then my last two classes were the usual school downers, especially social studies. The teacher started off sourly with a bunch of rules about getting papers in on time, not losing the assignment dittos or the textbooks, and showing up for every test or else. She acted like she expected half of us to mess up, and by the equally sour look on the kids' faces I guessed her expectations would come true.

I stopped in the girls' lavatory before I went to P.E. I found the gym easily enough by following my map of the campus. I knew I was a little late; still I wasn't so late the door would be locked.

I gave the knob a third yank and heard the class bell ring inside. I *was* locked out. Now what was I supposed to do? I stood there, hoping I wasn't sweating my new sweater. It was too hot to be wearing a sweater. But you can never tell about weather on September mornings. First it's foggy and then it's hot and then it rains. Piss! I yanked on the door viciously. It didn't even creak.

A hand touched the back of my shoulder, and I jumped away.

"It's only me," Craddoc said. "Don't freak."

"Ohh, oh, I didn't see you coming. I'm locked out." I sounded like an idiot.

"No, you're not." Craddoc took my hand. "You're at the wrong door. Let's go this way."

I followed him around the side of the building like a three-year-old baby. We passed some jocks in letter jackets, and one yelled, "Scoping out the frosh already?"

Craddoc just smiled and dropped my hand to drape an arm around my shoulders as he opened the double doors for me. "There's your class," he said.

I saw Sharon and Diane sitting on the gym floor with a group of girls and hurried in to join them without even thanking Craddoc. Smooth.

8

She's Pregnant

After school I had to check on my sister Robyn before I took off for Jenny's. Robyn's eleven years old, but Mama expects me to see that she comes home each day.

Jenny was shoving a casserole in the oven as I walked in her back door. "This is all I have to do tonight. Let's play some tunes."

Jenny's little brother, Kenneth, came in about that time and sidled across the kitchen, holding something behind him.

"What've you got?" Jenny asked.

"Nothing for you," Kenny said, backing down the hall.

Jenny went after him. "Let me see."

"No, no. I'm going to ask Daddy, not you." He slid into

his bedroom and locked the door before Jenny could get to him.

She gave up on Kenny, and we played her stereo and talked about boys until it was time for me to leave. Jenny assured me that Craddoc probably didn't even notice that I didn't thank him or say good-bye after he took me to P.E., but it still hassled my head, and I wished I could carry things off with guys as smoothly as she and Diane did.

In the morning, while we were sitting in home ec waiting for the bell, I asked Jenny what her brother had snuck into the house.

"Rats," Jenny said.

"Rats?" I said.

"A pair."

"Did your mother let him keep them?"

"Dad did "

"I've seen the white ones with pink eyes in pet shops."

The teacher, Mrs. Ash, moved to the front of the room with her roll sheet.

"These aren't white pink-eyed ones," Jenny said. "The female is a fat brown rat, and the male is a big black-and-white rat."

"Common brown rats?"

"That's right."

The bell rang. "Elsie Edwards? Sharon Hinkler?" Mrs. Ash called.

"Here," Sharon said.

"Here," I said.

"Today," Mrs. Ash told us, "we will learn how to make French toast."

Just awesome, I thought. I've only been making French toast since I was nine.

The next time I went over to Jenny's, Kenny brought the female rat into the living room and sat on the floor with it.

"Get that thing out of here," Jenny told him.

Kenny put out his hand and the rat obligingly crawled up his arm.

"Get it out of here," Jenny ordered.

"I don't have to." Kenny held up a piece of cheese and the rat curled around his neck, stretching its head out for a nibble.

Jenny planted herself in front of her brother. "Kenny, the deal was that you get to keep the rats as long as they are confined to your bedroom. You promised Mom."

"They aren't bothering her now," Kenny said.

"They're bothering us. Where's D.D.?"

"I put her out."

"Well, I'll let her in." Just as Jenny got to the door, there was a knock on the other side.

"Don't you dare let her in!" Kenny screamed.

Jenny opened the door to Jack and Craddoc.

"We saw Elsie headed this way and thought you could use some more company," Jack said. "But *who* don't you dare let in?"

11

"Oh, my cat," Jenny told him. "You can come in."

Jack and Craddoc came in and stood in the middle of the living room. I didn't know whether to get out of my chair and stand up to say hello or keep sitting down. It was the first time I'd seen Craddoc since the opening day of school. He was so prime-looking, with thick brown hair and brown eyes and broad shoulders and slim hips, I just smiled feebly because I couldn't think of anything to say.

"Sit down, you guys," Jenny said, "and I'll get some Cokes."

Jack sat on the davenport, and Craddoc sat beside Kenny on the floor. He took the rat off Kenny's neck and let her crawl up his own legs. After a minute of stroking the rat's body, he turned to me. "Hear you have first chair in choir. Knocked Leah down to second chair, huh?"

"Do you know Leah?" I asked him.

"It's hard not to." Then, as Jenny handed him a Coke, he looked up at her. "This rat's pregnant."

"Pregnant!" I thought Jenny was going to drop the other Cokes, so I got up to rescue my can. Jenny handed Jack his before sitting on the davenport beside him.

"This rat's pregnant!" Jenny repeated.

"That's right," Craddoc said, holding up the rat so we could see her bulging sides.

Kenny took his rat from Craddoc. "It doesn't matter if she has babies."

"You better keep the cat away from them," Jack told him.

12

"D.D. can stay outside," Kenny said.

"She will not," Jenny said.

Craddoc rose from the floor and came over to sit on the arm of my chair. "How come you call your cat D.D.?" he asked Jenny.

"Because she was a little slow learning to potty in the garden instead of on my mother's bed."

"And you complain about my rats!" Kenny said.

"Well, D.D. doesn't have baby rats," Jenny told him.

"Of course not. She always has baby cats."

"Bingo!" Jack said, and we all laughed.

That sort of relaxed everything, and I sank back in my chair. I'd been so conscious of Craddoc beside me that I hadn't moved a muscle since he'd sat down.

Craddoc put his arm across the back of the chair and leaned down toward me. So much for staying relaxed.

"And how about you?" he asked. "Dogs or cats or rats?"

"Nothing. My mother isn't the type."

"What type is she?"

"Mean," Kenny said, and gathered up his rat and headed for his room.

"And thank you, Mr. Tact," Jenny said, watching her brother leave. "Come on, you guys, it isn't raining for a change. Let's go out and shoot darts at the apple tree."

Jenny had a target nailed to her tree, and we all took turns throwing at it. We were about equally good, and it got boring after a while. Jack gathered up the darts and handed them to Jenny. "Now what?"

"Now I'd better split," I said. I wanted to be sure our house was perfect before Mama got home so she wouldn't have anything to rag at me about.

All of us trooped into Jenny's kitchen, and I got my coat.

"We better go, too," Craddoc told Jack. "And we can drop Elsie off."

His car was parked out in front, a little yellow VW convertible. I walked around and looked it over. "It smiles!"

"Ah, come on, Elsie." Jack climbed into the back seat.

Craddoc held the side door open for me. "I always thought it smiled. I think it's the way the hood curves."

I made a face at Jack before I got in. He hung over the front seat as Craddoc started up. "You know, Elsie, Craddoc has pets. He's going to enter his prize one in the school Olympics."

I looked at Craddoc. "What's your prize pet called?"

"Egglebeak Cluckerdink."

I thought a minute. "A chicken?"

"You got it," Jack said. "Old Egglebeak's going to win the Chicken Olympics next Tuesday."

I'd heard kids talking about the seniors' assembly, but I thought it was some kind of losers' race. When we pulled up at my house, Jack peered out the back window at our driveway. "Who owns the MG?"

"Mama," I said as I climbed out. The queasy feeling had settled in my stomach as soon as I saw she was home.

14

Robyn bounced out the front door and up to the car. "Mama's mad at you."

"What for?" I asked her.

"There were dishes all over the counter when she got in."

"Why didn't you put them in the dishwasher?"

Robyn carefully took in Craddoc, who'd come around to the curb. "I was busy," she told me.

"With what? Your Atari?" I nodded at Craddoc. "Thanks a lot for the ride."

He looked kind of surprised. I guess he'd expected me to invite him in or something, but cutting it short was better than risking Mama coming out and letting me have it in front of everybody.

The Chicken Olympics

Since Jack was in my second period English class, we walked down to the Chicken Olympics assembly together. I held my books against my chest as we weaved through the crowd in the gym. "Do you like Jenifer?" I asked Jack.

"She's a cute girl. Why do you want to know?"

I couldn't answer that I'd been primed by Jenny. "I just wondered."

He grinned at me. "You're pretty cute, too."

I spotted Jenny halfway up the bleachers in the freshman section, so I left Jack on the floor with his friends and climbed up to join her. The crowd had already begun to clap and chant by the time Diane arrived with Sharon tagging behind her. Diane settled beside me and took up the beat.

"RAINIER! Choo. Choo." Clap. Clap.

"COLD PACK! Choo. Choo." Clap. Clap.

"RAINIER! Choo. Choo." Clap. Clap.

"COLD PACK! Choo. Choo." Clap. Clap.

Sharon leaned over Diane's lap. "Here comes the vice principal. I bet he'll be mad."

Diane frowned. "What about?"

"Rainier's a beer," Sharon said.

"Noooo!" Diane raised her hands so Sharon had to move back in place.

"RAINIER! Choo. Choo." Clap. Clap.

"COLD PACK! Choo. Choo." Clap. Clap.

Leanne Elder, the student body president, moved up to the microphone on the gym floor. "Welcome to the first annual Chicken Olympics!"

The crowd roared.

"But first, please stand for the Pledge of Allegiance."

I stood up straight with my hand over my heart and, as I mumbled ". . . under God, indivisible . . ." I looked over Diane. She had on tan pants and a yellow blouse with a mandarin collar, and her black hair was cut short with bangs. The only popular things she wore were yellow socks rolled over the top edge of her tennis shoes. The cheerleaders rolled their socks just below their ankles, and I figured that's what Diane planned to be in this school, too.

When we took our seats, the lights dimmed until the gym was in darkness. A door opened on the side of the back wall behind the microphone, and a chicken-headed girl in a silver bathing suit ran out, holding a large Fourth of July sparkler high in the air. She circled the gym and went out the other door.

The lights came up, and Leanne announced into the microphone, "Here is Marty Taylor, our program chairman, who will give you the contest rules."

Marty got up to the microphone and sort of bobbed his head around shyly. "I want to welcome all of you to the first annual Fircrest High School Chicken Olympics!"

The crowd cheered; Sharon squealed, "Oh, excellent!"

"Now, the rules are," Marty went on, "that each contestant will be placed within the large circle on the floor out there. The representative from each club must stand outside the circle. The first contestant to cross the chalk line will be the winner. The winners of the first three heats will meet in a final runoff for the Golden Chicken Award!"

Loud cheers and a drum roll from the band, which was seated at the opposite end of the gym.

"The first contestant is Egg White and The Seven Yolks, sponsored by the drama club."

A red-faced girl came out of the side door holding a big white chicken at arm's length. More cheers.

"The second contestant is Drumstick, sponsored by the stage band."

A long drum roll and a saxophone blast for a banty hen.

"And the third contestant is Too Fried, sponsored by the sophomore class."

Loud cheers from the sophomore section.

"Now, will the representatives please place their contestants inside the circle and hold them until the flag drops, signaling the beginning of the first heat."

The kids put their chickens on the floor in the middle of the circle and held them there. The gym teacher, in a striped referee suit, crouched with one hand on the floor and the other hand pointing a flag to the ceiling.

"Silence, please," Marty said.

At the drop of the flag the representatives moved to the outside, leaving the chickens in the center of the circle placidly pecking at the corn on the floor. "Come on, Drumstick. Come on, Too Fried," the kids coaxed.

Drumstick moved a few inches away from the center, and the drummer banged on his drum. Too Fried flapped its wings, hopping a foot the other way, and the sophomores yelled encouragement. Egg White and The Seven Yolks wandered to the edge of the circle, and the referee dashed across the middle, grabbed the chicken, and held it high in the air just as Too Fried took off and flew into the stands. Sharon screamed as the chicken came down two rows behind us.

A boy climbed down the bleachers with Too Fried, while Marty announced, "The winner of the first heat is Egg White and The Seven Yolks!"

The drama kids whistled and clapped.

"Now," Marty said, "the first contestant in the second heat is Egglebeak Cluckerdink, sponsored by the athletic club."

Craddoc loped into the gym with a fat orange chicken.

"Yea, Craddoc!" the jocks yelled.

Diane breathed, "What a hunk!"

Just what I was thinking.

Sharon leaned across Diane toward me. "Wasn't that Craddoc who walked you to class the other day?"

Diane's eyes widened. "Craddoc Shaw?"

"I guess so," I said. "I don't know his last name."

"Oh?" She looked me over silently, and I could see she thought that if I didn't know his last name I must not really count.

I turned my attention to Marty, who was announcing Craddoc's competition, Six Peck and Chick and Chong. The chickens pecked at their corn forever until Craddoc's chicken finally edged outside the circle, and the jocks stomped and hollered as Egglebeak was raised in the air.

"Too excellent that Craddoc won," Sharon said. "Excellent" had been the in word in eighth grade.

Pica Beak, Pearly Gates, and Luchianni Peckeroni competed in the third heat. The typing club's Pica Beak won. The three heat winners held their chickens while Marty had the Golden Chicken Trophy displayed for the audience. The cheerleaders had been revving up the crowd, and now one of them joined Craddoc and petted his chicken.

"Who's that girl?" Sharon asked.

"Katie Bentler," Diane answered. "They'd make a cute couple."

I watched Katie pet the chicken in Craddoc's arms and look up into his face while she chattered away to him. Had Diane said, *"They'd make* a cute couple," or *"They make* a cute couple"? I shriveled into the little freshman Jack knew, somebody at Jenifer's house. Why would Craddoc like me?

"Will the representatives please place the contestants in the center of the ring for the final heat," Marty directed.

When the reps let go of the chickens, Pica Beak, Egg White, and Egglebeak milled around the circle for a long five minutes. Craddoc called and called to Egglebeak, but she ignored him and squatted down to clean her feathers. As soon as the corn was all eaten, Egg White made for the end of the gym and was declared the winner of the Golden Chicken Award.

"Too bad Craddoc lost." Jenny squeezed my arm. "You'll have to give him a consolation hug."

Out of the corner of my eye I caught Diane watching us. I was embarrassed to have her think I thought Craddoc liked me.

Sharon stood up, stepped down to the next row, and faced Diane. "That was *so* excellent!"

Diane sighed. "This is high school, Sharon. Get a new word."

The rest of us stood up and began jumping down the

bleachers with the crowd. As we trooped across the gym floor, I thought maybe I saw Craddoc spot me and move toward us, but I kept on walkin'.

I Hate You, Elsie Edwards

"Get up! Come on. *Get up!*" I bumped her mattress hard with my knee, and her head joggled on the pillow. "Get up, slug. Mama's going to be home in an hour and a half, and this house is going to be immaculate. So get up!" I rammed her mattress again.

"Get lost, Elsie," Robyn mumbled, keeping her eyes closed.

"O.K., slug, we'll do it the hard way."

I filled a pan of water at the kitchen sink and brought it back to Robyn's bedroom. "Now, either get out of that bed or I'm dumping this pan of water on your head."

She still didn't open her eyes. "You're not my boss. Get lost."

I tipped the pan and the quart of water streamed over her head.

Robyn tore out of her covers. "Elsie, you witch, you've soaked the bed. I'm calling Mama."

I followed her into the living room, stepping over the puddles she left on the floor. "You call Mama," I told her, "and the video player is going to get mysteriously broken. Think about it."

I took the pan into the kitchen and clunked it into the sink. Then I listened quietly to hear if she'd started dialing. Only stamping sounds going toward the bathroom. Good.

She came into the kitchen a few minutes later with her damp blond hair stuck to her head. "How do you think this is all going to get dry before Mama gets here?" she asked me as she stuffed a wad of wet sheets into the dryer.

"You can do it," I said. "And clean up the kitchen. I don't intend to get on restriction again because of your messes."

"I'm eating first." She opened the refrigerator and looked over the food.

I got the cleaning stuff from under the sink and carried it to the piano in the living room, dipped the bottle of polish over the rag, and started rubbing. When I wiped off the keys I was careful only the sounds of dissonance drifted into the kitchen. If I dared even one chord, Robyn would have an excuse to do nothing.

24

In an hour I had the living room, dining room, den, and two bathrooms done. I washed the sweat off my face before I went into the kitchen. It wasn't perfect, but at least everything was put away and the floor was waxed. I took up a container of Fantastik and sprayed the outside of the refrigerator.

Robyn stalked in. "Well, my room is all dry. No thanks to you. I'm going over to Cecile's."

"Good-bye," I said.

She stopped with her hand on the back doorknob. "You know I hate you, Elsie Edwards."

"It's mutual," I called after her.

I was sweeping off the back porch when Mama drove up. She carried the groceries in. I put the broom away and started emptying the bags she placed on the counter.

"Jenny called and invited me over. Her folks are going out to dinner." I held out a slip of paper. "Here's the number. Mrs. Sawyer's home now, if you want to check."

Mama ignored the paper. "What about . . ." She hesitated. This was Saturday and my week of restriction was up. "What do you expect Robyn to do? I might be going out."

"You could drop her off at Dad's." I watched her face carefully. She'd hate the suggestion, I knew, but what could she say?

She shrugged and reached into the cupboard for a glass.

"Mrs. Sawyer will bring me home after they get back."

She shrugged again. I waited a minute and then slipped away for a shower.

Jenny's mom and dad were about to leave when I got to her house

"Now, remember"—Mrs. Sawyer stooped over Jenny's chair to kiss her good-bye—"no boys in the house."

"There won't be," Jenny assured her. "But if somebody comes over before dark, can we at least have them out in the yard?"

"I thought you invited Elsie for company," Mr. Sawyer said.

"All I asked was to let other friends in the yard to be polite. We're not nuns."

Mrs. Sawyer picked up her purse. "I guess that's all right. Just don't forget, Kenny's part of the gang tonight."

"Darn," Jenny said. "I was going to lock him in his room with his rats."

"Hey!" Kenny objected.

"Only kidding," Jenny told him.

As soon as her parents were out the door, Jenny hopped out of her chair. "Let's make a cake in case the boys do come over. The pizza Mom left won't be enough."

Jenny was spreading the frosting over the cake and I was chopping nuts for the topping when the knock on the front door came.

"You get it, Kenny," Jenny told him.

Kenny tossed the spoon he was licking into the sink and

took off. We heard the door open, then Jack's voice, then Kenny's voice. "You can't come in the house because Mom's gone. You can only come in the yard until it's dark. Go around the back."

Jenny hurriedly swirled the last of the frosting over the sides of the cake. "I hope they don't tell him to shove it." She put the knife down and ran her fingers through her long brown hair. "How do I look?"

"Great," I said. "How do I look?"

"As usual," Jenny said. "Like a thin Dolly Parton."

"Sure," I said, sprinkling the nuts over the frosting.

"You do, really," Jenny insisted. "With your blond curly hair and blue eyes and dimple. Craddoc sure notices."

"Me and Katie and Diane."

Jenny put the bowls in the sink. "Don't be stupid, Elsie. Craddoc doesn't even know Diane. You have more trouble believing someone likes you."

Kenny dashed through the kitchen and opened the back door.

Jack poked his head in and Craddoc leaned over his shoulder. "Is it legal to put our toes on the floor? Somebody's birthday?"

"No. Dinner." Jenny finished running water in the mixing bowls and wiped her hands on the dish towel.

"Ask us to dinner," Jack said.

"If you want to eat out on the picnic table."

They wanted to. We played darts first, Kenny firmly

keeping his place in line as "part of the gang." The pizza went fast, and I was glad we had the cake. Jack ate most of it.

"What ever happened to Marianne?" he asked me as he cut himself his third slice. "I haven't seen her around for a couple of years."

"She moved to Denver in the seventh grade."

"Who was Marianne?" Craddoc asked.

"A girl who was nice to me when everybody else hated me."

That did it. Total silence.

"Marianne was a good kid," Jack finally said. "You want us to carry the dishes in?"

Kenny helped the boys clear the table, and Jenny went in to get her dad's horseshoe set. Craddoc beat us all at the game. It was a warm evening for the end of September, and after three rounds I flopped down on my back under the apple tree to cool off. Craddoc flopped beside me, and Jenny and Jack settled in the covered swing.

Kenny planted himself in the middle of the yard. "What am I supposed to do?"

"Go get my felt pens and draw on the picnic table," Jenny told him.

Craddoc stared up through the leaves in the tree. "Saturday afternoons are the best ones in the fall. I never get to see anybody after school because of turnouts."

"Wh-what position do you play?" I asked.

"Kicker. I'm the guy who comes in for one minute on a

fourth down to boot the ball down the field."

"That's all?"

"Well, if there's a touchdown I try to make the extra point."

"That can win a game, can't it?"

"Oh, sometimes." He rolled over to look at me. "What's all this about kids hating you?"

"I was fat. And I ate their lunches and their candy and anything else I could get my hands on."

"A compulsive eater?"

"You could say that."

"Why?"

I put my arms over my eyes and stared into my skin. "My dad found some other lady and my mother was upset, which is an understatement. She had to take care of my sister, who was two, and I was a bother to her. So she fed me cookies to shut me up. First, I ate because I felt bad, and then I just ate all the time." I snorted into my arms. "I guess I felt bad all the time. And the fatter I got the lonelier I got because everybody hated me—or something like that."

"Hmmm, you're so good-lookin' it's hard to imagine anyone hating you." Craddoc pulled my arms away from my face. "And how do you feel now?"

"I'm O.K. now." I kept my eyes turned away from his, though, as I said it. I was afraid the trembling inside me would show on my face.

"I'm not so sure about that," he said as he bent

down and kissed me gently on the lips.

"It's getting dark," Kenny announced loudly. "So I'm going in the house now."

"What a darling little brother you have," I heard Jack tell Jenny.

Sorry Doesn't Mean Anything

Sunday, Monday, and Tuesday mornings I woke up feeling like I had a secret Christmas present. I stretched in my bed and smiled at the ceiling and planned over and over what I'd wear Friday night with Craddoc. I thanked the lovely luck that had helped Mama sell a duplex on Sunday, which made her so high she didn't care what night I went out. She usually went out on Fridays with her office staff, and I couldn't have suggested Dad's for Robyn again, but this time Mama said, "No problem."

Monday morning Craddoc walked me to first period and stood at the door of the home ec room asking me what show I'd like to see. Sharon almost cracked her head on the door jamb watching us instead of her big feet. Later

Jenny asked me if Craddoc had kissed me Saturday, and I said yes, had Jack kissed her? She said sort of, but it was no big deal.

Second period on Monday the English teacher was late to class. Jack came into the room, took in her absence, sauntered over to the phone on the classroom wall, and picked up the receiver. "Two bacon burgers to go, French fries, and a chocolate milk shake," he said, and hung up.

That got a little laugh.

The English teacher, Miss Bickford, arrived and looked suspiciously around at the smiling faces. She sobered us up fast with her assignment on semicolons, main clauses, and coordinate elements.

On Tuesday Jack was late to class. Miss Bickford had already called the roll, and I didn't see her change the roll sheet after he walked in. On Wednesday he was a little late again. Miss Bickford said, "That makes two absences for you, Jack. You know you're allowed only ten in a semester."

"Two *absences*," Jack said, "for being two minutes late?"

"Absences and tardies are counted the same. Ten and you're in a no-credit situation in the class."

"I never heard of anything like that," Jack protested.

"Then I take it you haven't read your student handbook." She turned her back on him and began passing out copies of *Great Expectations*.

"That's crazy," Jack mumbled, walking to his seat.

32

Miss Bickford whirled around. "I won't tolerate insolence in my classroom. You go down and sit in the vice principal's office for the hour."

Jack stormed out of the room; Miss Bickford put down the books and went for the wall phone. "I've sent Jack Hanson down to see Mr. Piker. Please tell him Jack was late to class, insolent to me, and he just left, slamming the door. I won't tolerate this, and I want him out of my class." She turned to us after she left the phone. "You ninth graders can straighten up and start acting like high school students right now."

I put out both my hands. "But he was really only two minutes late."

"When the bell rings you are in your seat ready to work."

I gave a big sigh and opened the book on my desk.

"All right, Elsie, you can go down and keep Jack company."

"But . . ."

"Go ahead."

I slammed the door, too.

Mr. Piker talked to Jack and me for twenty minutes on how to behave like a high school student. "Now," he said, "I expect you to be back in that class tomorrow, *on time*, with your pencils out and your mouths shut."

That didn't seem too bad. He really didn't even seem mad about the whole thing. Jack and I got up to go.

Mr. Piker reached for his phone. "I'll explain to your parents why you weren't in class today."

"That's it for me," I told Jack while we were walking down to the commons. "There goes Friday night and every Friday night for the next month. If I'm lucky."

"I'm sorry, Elsie."

"It isn't your fault. It's my mouth."

I was jumpy all day, and I could barely eat the dinner I fixed for Robyn and me. Mama came in just as we finished. She stood in the middle of the kitchen, eyeing me at the table.

"That was a very nice call I had at *the office* today. *With everybody* listening."

"I'm sorry. I . . ."

"Sorry doesn't mean anything. You've been sorry for years. And I'm going to tell you just one time. I am *not* going to be running up to that high school to be told about a bunch of crap you've pulled. I am *not*. Do you understand?"

"Yes." I fiddled with my fork while she watched me. "Uh . . . would you like me to warm you up some dinner?"

"No, I would not. Just do me a favor and get out of my sight."

I did. Fast.

Wednesday night I got Robyn's and my dinner, ate, got the kitchen cleaned up, and was in my room studying before Mama got home. Thursday the same. She hadn't said anything about restricting me and I wasn't going to be around to remind her.

I passed Craddoc in the commons before school Friday morning. He didn't notice me. He and some of the other football players were talking to the cheerleaders who were decked out in short, short dresses that came just below their hips, nylon tights, rolled socks, and tennis shoes. If a regular student dressed like that, she'd be sent home Katie Bentler had her hands on Craddoc's arm, looking up at him, talking away.

Sharon joined me at the commons doors. "Craddoc's certainly occupied this morning."

I didn't answer.

"What are you going to do tonight?" she wanted to know.

"Go to a show," I said. "Maybe."

I didn't talk to anybody on the ride home from school. I was glad, for once, that Jenny rode another bus. I didn't talk to Robyn, either, when I got home. I washed my hair, took my lavender wool turtleneck out of the closet and hung it on the doorknob, then started dinner. The kitchen clock hung on the minutes as I picked at my food. What if he just didn't show?

"You're going out with that Craddoc guy tonight," Robyn said.

"So?"

"What a weird name."

I heard Mama's car in the driveway, and my chest tightened. I stood up and began clearing my place.

"Hey, wait a minute," Robyn said. "I haven't even finished."

I was at the sink rinsing off my plate when she came in. The phone rang in the living room, and she walked through the kitchen to answer it.

"It's for you, Elsie," she called back.

"Hello," I said.

"This is Craddoc," he said. "Uh, Elsie, my grandmother came today, and my mom asked me to stay around tonight and visit with her. If you don't mind."

"All right," I said.

"I hope I haven't wrecked your Friday night. She's leaving Sunday, and I'll give you a call then, O.K.?"

"Don't bother," I said, and hung up.

I lay on my bed in the dark with my arm over my eyes and the hot tears rolling down the sides of my face. Robyn opened the door. "It's the phone again for you."

"Get out of here."

"It's Craddoc."

"Get out of here and hang the phone up." I turned over toward the wall and took a long shuddering breath.

The house became quiet, and our grandfather clock bonged twelve, and one, two, and three. I don't remember hearing four, so I must have fallen asleep for a few hours. I woke up with Mama standing over me in her nightgown. "It's *Mrs. Shaw* on the phone now. Get up and answer it."

I trailed dopily out to the phone, my head swimming. Mrs. Shaw?

"Hello," I said.

"Elsie, this is Juanita Shaw, Craddoc's mother. I hope I didn't get you up."

"No, that's O.K." I looked at the clock standing against the wall. Five after nine.

"The reason I called . . . Well, I have two reasons. The first is to invite you to Sunday dinner, if you'd like to come. And the second is to explain why I asked Craddoc to stay home last night."

"Oh, that's O.K. It didn't matter."

"I think it mattered to Craddoc. You see, his grandmother isn't well. She may not be with us very long, and Craddoc is her only grandchild."

"Oh."

"She'd very much like to meet you. May I send Craddoc over about four tomorrow afternoon to pick you up?"

I was dripping with embarrassment, but I couldn't think of any way to say no, so I choked out another stupid "O.K."

She said she'd see me Sunday, then. I said good-bye and sagged into the chair by the telephone.

Trust Me

I picked through my closet for the fifth time. The cream-colored skirt I'd planned to wear had a grease smear on the side. I'd scrubbed it with Energine and finally soap and water, but the grease still showed. Trying to hurry made me so nervous I caught myself in the old habit of tugging on my hair.

Enough of that. I yanked my old navy blue skirt and lavender sweater out of the closet and pulled them on. Shoes. I had a choice of tan high heels, brown loafers, blue moccasins, white tennis shoes, or black boots. The moccasins were the only things that even came close.

Mama appeared at my bedroom door. "Craddoc's still here."

"I know."

She looked me over as I put on my jacket. "Those shoes don't do anything for that outfit."

"I've tried every pair I have. What do you think I've been doing in here?" She always makes me feel so clunky. "I don't want to go anyway."

"It's a little late for that."

She left, and I went into the bathroom. Anytime I'm visiting someplace new, I think I have to go as soon as I get out of my house, and I didn't want to walk into Craddoc's and ask, "Where's the bathroom?"

When I finished, Mama was in the hall holding a pair of gray pumps. "Here. Try these."

I tried them on in front of my bedroom mirror. They fit perfectly. "What if I get a spot on them?"

"You'd better not," she said. "And you better speed it up. Craddoc's been waiting fifteen minutes."

Craddoc kept his attention on the road as we drove to his house. Things didn't feel so easy between us.

"What did you and Mama talk about while you were waiting?" I asked him.

"Mostly about business. My uncle's a real estate broker, and your mom knows him, and she's heard of my dad's construction company."

"Your uncle sells houses, too?"

"No, business properties." He headed the car down the road leading to Woodway.

"Mama thinks that's where the money is. I guess she'd like to sell business property."

"That's what she said."

"What's the matter with your grandmother?"

"She has polyarteritis."

"Is that like arthritis?"

"No. I don't know exactly what it is. She has trouble breathing and looks kind of skinny and weak. It's too bad. She's a neat lady."

If I told him I was sorry about his grandmother being sick, it would sound funny after I wouldn't believe she existed. I concentrated on telling myself my bladder was *not* full. Craddoc wound his car down the Woodway roads, which were bordered by evergreen trees and rhododendrons. He eased into his long, wooded driveway, pulled the car up in the middle of a turnaround, and helped me out.

I entered his living room wondering if my hair looked all right and how I could ask to go to the bathroom. Craddoc's mother and father got up to greet us, while his grandmother smiled from the davenport. When the introductions were over, Mr. Shaw offered me a glass of wine, and Craddoc's grandmother patted the seat beside her. "Come sit with me, dear."

I sat down, carefully balancing my wine glass.

"What a lovely sweater you're wearing. I'm very fond of lavender." She reached out a thin hand and fingered my collar. "*So*, you didn't believe Craddoc when he told you he had to baby-sit his old grandmother."

Unfortunately at that moment I was taking my first sip of wine. I wiped my chin with the back of my hand while the old lady laughed.

"I didn't blame you a bit. When I heard him, 'Uh, Elsie,' over the telephone I thought to myself, 'That girl's never going to believe that.' It sounded like all the cock-and-bull stories men tell women."

"What's that?" Mr. Shaw said, putting down his wine glass.

"Yeah, what's that?" Craddoc chimed in. He didn't have any wine. Fall training. "I don't tell cock-and-bull stories."

"No, you don't," his grandmother agreed. "That's why I love you so much."

Mrs. Shaw left for the kitchen and came right back and stood at the dining room door. "Dinner will be ready in three minutes."

"Oh!" I said, quick like a fox. "Could you show me where the lavatory is so I could wash up?"

The dinner was good—roast lamb and vegetables and chocolate cake—but the conversation was pretty boring. Craddoc got asked how he thought the Fircrest team would do in the league this year, and I got asked how I liked high school. I noticed the grandmother took little helpings and only picked at her food. Nobody commented, and she never whined about how she felt, like my grandma would have done.

"Your grandmother *is* neat," I told Craddoc when the evening was over and we were walking back to his car. "And she sure likes you."

"Yep," Craddoc agreed. "She got my dad to name me after her father."

"Oh, I wondered. . . ."

Craddoc didn't drive all the way off his property. He veered to the right and went down a side lane and turned off the car lights.

"Now, I think we should have a little talk." My throat caught at the "don't mess with me" tone in his voice. "It burned me when you brushed me off. I don't tell cock-and-bull stories."

"I know, but . . . most people don't have to stay home every night when a grandmother visits for three days."

"Most people don't have a grandmother as sick as mine."

"You didn't tell me that part."

"That's right. I didn't." He changed channels on the radio until he found a rock station that was playing music instead of commercials. "Look, Elsie, I think if two people like each other enough to want to be together, they should be able to trust each other. Don't you?"

"Yes," I murmured.

"I trust you. Can you trust me?"

"Yes," I murmured again.

He tipped my head up and kissed me softly once, then kissed me again, holding me so tight that I didn't know if I was breathless from the hug or from the kiss.

The Killer Game

When I was with Craddoc I didn't feel stupid about being a freshman, but most of the juniors, and even the sophomores, didn't treat us that way. The principal came on the P.A. system and announced that he would not tolerate any freshman initiations, for all the good that did. Jack got it worse than most. Not because he wasn't liked, but because he was the kind of person all twelve hundred kids in the school knew about inside of a month.

For a change, Jack was on time to English class after our visit to the vice principal's office. Every day, in fact, for two weeks—until one Wednesday when he came in forty minutes late. Miss Bickford was ragging at him so hard she could barely stop to read the note he handed

43

her. He stood in front of the room with a "she doesn't know what she's doing" look on his face until she finished with the note and waved him to his seat.

As we walked out of class together after the bell rang, I asked him where he'd been.

"In the john."

"For forty minutes!"

"Forty minutes," he agreed. "Some friend of Craddoc's told me he wanted to show me something, so I followed him into the can, and we were standing there, and he waited until I couldn't move, and then he split and locked the outside door."

"Why couldn't you move?"

"Duh! Why do you think?"

"Oh. Well, who got you out?"

"The janitor. The vice principal gave me the note for Bickford."

"Bickford sure has a short fuse."

"She doesn't even have a fuse," Jack said. "Just a rip cord tied to her chair, and every time she gets up she loses it."

We were all the way to the choir room by then, so I went into the class laughing and Jack went on down the hall. Actually, I thought Jack was lucky he didn't get his head stuck in a toilet bowl or get himself taped to a tree. The girls got it, but not as bad as the guys.

It was usually during P.E. that we were teased. On sunny days we played baseball out on the field and met the seniors' elective P.E. class coming in. Our group was walking off the field that day when I noticed brown fringe on Diane's ring finger and asked her about it.

"It's upholstery fringe. Mom was sewing it on a pillow, and I picked up a scrap and twisted it around my finger. It looked neat so I sewed myself a ring. Do you want me to make you one?" Diane had been putting herself out for me ever since she figured that I was really going with Craddoc.

"No, that's O.K.," I told her. I thought the fringe looked neat, too, but I didn't want to be copying Diane. That obviously didn't bother Sharon, though, because she grabbed Diane's outstretched hand and examined the ring closely.

About that time the seniors moved in near us with archery bows and arrows. "Get your arrows ready!"

"Oh, it's for the little people!" They placed the arrows in their bows as if to shoot us.

"Ready, aim, fire!"

Diane laughed, but I could see she didn't get off on being called "the little people."

The first football game was Friday night at Everett. Diane said her cousin was driving up and Jenny was going with them and did I want to go, too.

"Sure," I said. "Pick me up at Jenny's."

Sharon moved in close to Diane. "I really wouldn't want to miss that game." It didn't do her any good. Diane wasn't about to include her.

When I got to Jenny's house Friday night, I found her great-aunt and uncle had dropped in for a visit. I had barely gotten seated when the old aunt put her nose up in the air. "What *is* that smell?"

"Yes, Kenny," Jenny said.

Kenny stopped eyeing the packages by his great aunt's chair and left for his bedroom. When he came back he announced reassuringly, "They just needed some fresh paper in their cage."

"What did?" the uncle asked.

"Oh, Kenny has some little pets," Mrs. Sawyer said. "Tell us where you're going next on your trip."

"We're going up to Vancouver tonight and then over to Victoria tomorrow." The uncle looked at his watch. "And we'd better get going. I don't like driving in the dark."

"Yes, we better," his wife agreed. "Here. I brought you a little present, Jenny. And you a little present, Kenny."

Jenny opened hers first. It was seven nylon underpants with the day of the week embroidered on the seat of each pair. Kenny waited politely for Jenny to say how darling they were and then tore the wrapping off his present, stared at the gray shirt in the box, and sat back dejectedly. "Just what I hate! Another crummy shirt."

"Ken-*ney!*" Mrs. Sawyer whispered angrily.

The great-aunt rose stiffly from her chair, and Jenny kissed her good-bye. "I love the panties, Auntie. Thank you so much."

As soon as the door closed on her relatives, Jenny turned

to her brother. "Way to go, Kenny." And then she said to me, "Come on, Elsie. I gotta get my jacket. Diane should be here any minute."

I followed her into the bedroom with Mrs. Sawyer right behind us. Mrs. Sawyer brushed the cat off Jenny's bed and sat down. "*Guess* what happened to me today?"

"You're pregnant," Jenny guessed.

"Nope."

"You got a raise," I guessed.

"Ummm, that's part."

It was an easy guess. She looked like a balloon ready to pop.

"O.K." Jenny sat down on one side of her and I sat on the other. "We give up. What happened to you today?"

Mrs. Sawyer clapped her hand to her chest. "*I* am the new manager of the EverBloom Nursery."

"You're kidding," Jenny said.

"No, I'm not. The owner took me out to lunch today and asked me. I'm to take over the first of November."

"How much money are you going to make?"

"More than your dad."

Jenny's face turned thoughtful, and she chipped at her nail polish until her mother bent down and looked in her face. "Aren't you happy for me?"

"Sure I am." Jenny hugged her mother, and when her mother gave her a hug back she put her arm around me and included me in it. Some people are lucky with their mothers, and some aren't so lucky.

Loud honking sounded outdoors. "Awk! Diane." Jenny grabbed her jacket and told her mother see ya later, and we dashed out to the car. Jenny and I piled into the back seat, and Diane's cousin took off, burning about an inch of rubber. As she careened around a corner heading for I-5, Diane leaned over the seat. "It took you guys long enough."

"We were talking to my mom," Jenny explained. "She just got made manager of the nursery where she works."

"Aw right!" Diane said. "You'll get a credit card at Nordstrom's!"

"Don't I wish. What bothers me is how my dad's going to feel when Mom one-ups him with her paycheck."

Diane's cousin maneuvered the car onto the freeway. "Women are equal now, and some of them are more equal."

"The only difference I see is that the slavery has been shoved off on us young women." Jenny turned to me. "How did you escape your chains tonight?"

"I lucked out," I said. "Robyn got invited to a slumber party."

The stadium was packed when we got to Everett, and we had to climb up to the top of the stands to find an empty space wide enough for the four of us. Diane led the way with her cousin following. "You sit here, Linda." Diane moved down one place, leaving room for her cousin. I sat on the other side of Diane with Jenny beside me.

Linda had a car blanket, and we spread it along our

laps. I kicked the bottom of the blanket so it would hang down over my legs, and I accidentally hit the head of the man in front of me. He turned around, and I hunched up my shoulders. "Sorry about that."

There was a roll of drums, the cheerleaders leaped into the air, and the announcer said, "Here comes the Fircrest team!" He called out each player's name as the team trotted across the field, and we clapped hard for "Shaw, number 18."

Craddoc placed the ball carefully on the tee and backed up for the kickoff. I held my breath. Make it a long one, Craddoc. Make it a long one. He did, and the crowd cheered, and I relaxed.

There was no score in the first quarter, and Craddoc didn't get back in. There was no score in the second quarter either, and the bench we were sitting on was getting miserable by the time the gun sounded, ending the half. The band marched out to the field and formed a big F, and the cheerleaders yelled, "Gimme an F. Gimme an I . . ."

"Which cheerleader do you think is the best?" Diane asked.

"Oh, the one next to the end on the right," Linda said.

Jenny agreed, and Diane agreed, and I said nothin'. That was Katie Bentler, and I didn't like her being the best anything.

The second half was the same as the first, with the teams just pushing each other back and forth down the field. I wiggled around on the wooden bench and watched the big clock, which was forever stopping. When the clock had seven minutes remaining, the loudspeaker blared, "Fourth down, and Shaw is coming into the game."

Jamison, the quarterback, held the ball pointed to the ground, and Craddoc backed down the field. I sat up and took another big breath. Craddoc ran forward, made the kick, and the ball sailed over the goalposts.

"It's good!" Diane screamed.

"A thirty-four-yard field goal by Shaw," the loudspeaker boomed. "Fircrest leads 3–0."

As I came down from a leap in the air, I heard the man in front of me say, "That kid's a genius."

The field goal was the only score of the game, and when the gun sounded at the end of the second half, our team ran to the sidelines and slapped Craddoc on the bottom. Diane and Jenny and Linda and I hugged each other and yelled, "Fun and joy!"

"What'll we do now?" Linda asked when things calmed down. "Why don't we go get Craddoc and take him with us?" Same old Linda, always on the hunt.

"We can't." Diane started climbing over the benches. "He has to ride back on the bus with the team."

I pushed through the crowd to keep up with her. "Craddoc told me to meet him at the A and W."

"Off to the A and W," Diane called.

"Where's the A and W?" Linda called back.

"We'll show you." Diane moved a little kid out of her

way and hopped down the last three benches.

We were sitting in the car, drinking our root beer floats, when Craddoc drove up in his yellow Volkswagen. He parked two lanes down from us, and there was a bunch of yelling when he got out of his car.

"Hey, Craddoc, way to go, man!"

"That was a killer, Shaw!"

"That's Craddoc?" The root beer glass sagged in Linda's hand. "Gawd, he's beautiful!"

Craddoc opened the back door of Linda's station wagon and reached for my hand.

"That kick was awesome," Diane told him.

He smiled at Diane and pulled me out of the car. I looked back as Craddoc led me away. "I guess I'll see you all later."

"Well," Craddoc said, holding his keys over the steering wheel, "do you know a secluded little spot where we can talk?"

"You'll find one," I said, and snuggled into the Volkswagen seat, feeling like Princess Diana who'd just taken off with Charles.

Green Eyes

I got up the next morning riding high, until Robyn told me at the breakfast table that Dad had called and wanted me to baby-sit.

"When did Jeanne have her baby?" I asked Robyn.

"Two weeks ago." Robyn kept up on Dad's new family. I never did. "He said for you to call him back as soon as you were awake."

Mama was at the sink unloading the dishwasher and didn't seem to be paying attention to the conversation, so I talked loudly to her. "He wouldn't have anything to do with me when I was fat. Now that I'm old enough to take care of his kid, he wants me to baby-sit!"

"Don't tell me about it," she said. "I don't care if you go or not."

Robyn gathered up her dishes. "I'd do it if he'd let me. He said he'd pay you ten dollars for the day."

That was a whole new ball game. I finished my breakfast and went to the phone.

The baby-sitting at Dad's was pretty easy, since the baby slept most of the time. I did the dishes and cleaned up the kitchen. Jeanne is a bit of a slob. I thought her stomach would have gone down more after she had the baby, but her skirt looked like it was stretched over a hamper. Before they left Dad tried to kiss me good-bye, and I backed off. He could have made my life easier when I was a miserable little kid if he had wanted to put himself out, and I wasn't about to forget it.

Jeanne beat Dad to the door when they returned. She had two wet spots on her blouse, and she snatched up the sleeping baby, settled on the davenport, and had that thing nursing before it got its eyes open. Dad didn't try to kiss me again. I thanked him for the ten dollars and split.

The money was handy when we started on a clothing unit the next week in home ec. I bought black material and a pattern for a witch's costume to wear to Diane's Halloween party. Jenny picked out a blouse to sew because she already had her mother's belly dancer costume.

Sharon came by my sewing table and looked over my pattern. "That's neat. I think I'll go as a white witch."

I snatched the pattern back. "Think up your own ideas." She didn't, of course, which pissed me off.

Jenny and I both had a terrible time fitting sleeves into

53

armholes. I don't really know how anybody can get them in without puckering. Mrs. Ash made us do ours over three times.

I was bent over my material, pinning the collar, when there was a big commotion at Sharon's table. Jenny and I went over to see what was the matter. There was Sharon trapped with her finger against the sewing machine needle. She'd sewn the finger fringe she'd copied from Diane to the costume she'd copied from me. I went back to my seat, smiling, while Mrs. Ash cut her loose, telling her what a stupid thing it was to wear something like that on her finger when she was using an electric machine.

I tried the witch costume on at home the morning of the party and asked Robyn what she thought. Robyn screwed up her face, figuring out her answer. "Well, I think it's O.K., but it needs something more. Why don't you get some of that trimming with the little balls hanging on it and sew it to the end of your sleeves? And get some black paper, too, and I'll make you a pointed hat. And get a box of silver stars and paste them around the hem."

"Hmmm." I stood in front of the bathroom door mirror, visualizing Robyn's suggestions. Robyn may be spoiled rotten, but she isn't dumb. "You got any money?" I asked her.

"A little bit," she answered cautiously. "What happened to your ten dollars?"

"I spent it. Listen, give me what you have and I'll pay

you back the next time I baby-sit for Dad. I told him I'd do it again."

Robyn forked up the money, and I went off to the store while she made a hat pattern on newspapers. I bagged the silver star idea but got the ball trim and the black paper. By the time I got back, Robyn was sitting on the living room floor waiting for me with the pattern, scissors, and sewing basket beside her. She had Mama's old Rolling Stones records on, and we sang together as we worked, Robyn on the hat and me on the sleeves. When Jenny got to my house late in the afternoon, I put the costume on again, and she and Robyn agreed I looked awesome.

Jenny and I went over to Diane's early to help her with the decorations. It was a cold, dark, misty evening, perfect for a murder. We walked down the middle of the street, giggling and pushing each other toward the hulking bushes along the sidewalk as we spotted oncoming cars.

Diane was lugging her stereo down to the rec room when we came in her door. We shed our coats, and I got up on the pool table to fasten the crepe paper to the ceiling, while Jenny covered the lamps with papier mâché pumpkins. We stashed cans of Coke in a garbage can full of ice, put bowls of popcorn around, and cranked up the stereo. When we were finished, we sat on the rec room floor eating hot dogs and congratulating each other on how prime the place looked.

People started piling in about eight-thirty. Sharon came

in her white witch costume, which I was happy to see sagged in all the wrong places. Katie Bentler came in a cat costume, which I was unhappy to see fit skintight in all the right places. Jack arrived, looking a little red-eyed under his white clown makeup. Craddoc came as a bum with a bowler hat on the back of his head and half a cigar in his mouth. Katie ran up to him, put her paws on his chest, and licked his cheek, and he laughed and pulled her cat's tail which started me off so pissed I could barely say hello.

Craddoc barely said hello back before Jamison brought him a pool cue and said he challenged Craddoc to a game. I sort of milled around, going upstairs for more popcorn and dancing once with Jack. I ended up sitting down with Sharon and talking to her for one solid half hour about nothin'. Craddoc finally came over and perched on the arm of the couch. He had time to tilt my witch's hat over my eyes and tell me the party was a killer before Katie tugged on his arm, saying she needed a partner.

"You come, too," he told me as she dragged him away.

"I don't know how to play," I said.

He went with Katie anyway, of course. I watched the pool game through the crowd, and when Katie jumped up and hugged Craddoc, I knew the game was over and they'd won. He put his cue on the rack and I thought, At last. Just as I got off the couch to meet him, I saw him grab Katie's tail and pull her out in the middle of the floor to dance.

That did it. I walked past Sharon's knowing look, out the rec room door, and up the stairs to the living room, where I picked up my coat. Diane's mother turned away from the TV to ask me, "Leaving so soon?"

"Yes," I said, putting on my coat. "Tell Diane thanks for the party."

Nobody was home when I got there. Robyn was at the haunted house with Cecile, and Mama was out on the town, I guess. I sat at the kitchen table and stared at the clock. Twenty-five after ten. Twenty-six after ten. The house was cold. What would he do when he found out I was gone? I could go back to Diane's and say I just went for a walk. A picture of him pulling Katie onto the dance floor swam up in my head, and I blinked back my tears.

The phone rang.

I picked up the receiver slowly.

"What's going on?" Craddoc asked.

"I don't know. What's going on?"

"Well, you left."

"I didn't think you'd notice."

"Ah, come off it, Elsie. You danced with Jack. This was supposed to be a party."

I stood still, holding the receiver.

"I'll come get you," Craddoc said.

"What for? So I can pass you and Katie the popcorn bowl?"

"Elsie, this is stupid."

"Well, maybe I'm stupid," I said, and hung up.

I walked around the living room, shivering. Last chance, I said to myself. Last chance, stupid. I lay in bed for hours. I couldn't get warm. I couldn't fall asleep. All I could do was reach under my pillow for the wet Kleenex and smear away my tears. And remember a song that Jeff, an old boyfriend of Mama's, taught me.

Jeff used to bring race records over to our house to play. I didn't even know what a race record was until he explained that they were records black people played for themselves in the thirties. I always liked Jeff, and Mama did for a while. Mama can be fun when she has something going for herself. Anyway, what I heard in my head that night was the blues tune, "Sun gonna shine in my back door someday . . ."

In the morning I listened to the sounds of the rain on my window and then the sound of Robyn in the shower. She opened my door a crack. "Are you awake yet?"

I turned my aching head on the pillow, and she came in and sat on my bed. "How did the costume go over?"

"The *costume* went over great."

"Ohh. Trouble with Craddoc again?"

"Right."

"Too bad. He's some hunk."

"That's the trouble. Everybody thinks he's a hunk."

Robyn thought that over. "I guess that could be a problem all right. It's funny, you and Mama are so pretty you wouldn't think you'd have trouble with guys. Well, I'll be over at Cecile's if you need anything."

58

I watched her go out the door. She'd been nice, for a change. It's true Mama and I look alike. I never considered before how Robyn felt about that.

As soon as I got to the sewing room Monday, Jenny jumped on me. "What *is* going on? Where were you yesterday? I called you four times."

"I walked down to the beach." I put my purse and books below the sewing table and lowered my weary body onto the bench.

"You sure look down. What happened between you and Craddoc anyway?"

"Nothing. Did he say anything?"

"The first I knew he was going around asking everybody if they'd seen you. Then I saw him talking to Sharon. After that he must have split. How come you left the party?"

"I got tired of sitting alone."

"And you walked out on Craddoc just because he played pool for a while?"

"Played with Katie Bentler, you mean."

"Oh, Elsie. Katie comes on to all the guys. She's harmless."

"To whom?" I jerked the black scraps out of my sewing box and got up and dumped them in the wastebasket, came back to my seat, and listened to Mrs. Ash's dumb lecture on color coordination.

An hour later Jack started in.

"Back off," I told him. "I've already heard how mean I

was to poor Craddoc. Katie Bentler will console him."

"Elsie, he wouldn't like an air-head like Katie Bentler. Have you ever heard her jabber?"

No, I hadn't. And I wondered the rest of the day, *was* she an air-head?

For dinner I took boxes of Stouffer's Lean Cuisine out of the freezer. As I ripped off the cardboard covers, the tiny idea that I could call Craddoc and say I was sorry grew in my head. It would just be a few awful minutes of embarrassment, and I could explain that I was coming over to dance with him when he grabbed Katie, and I had been disappointed. . . . No. The best thing to do was just to say I was sorry.

I stuffed the aluminum pans into the oven and went into the living room. I took a long breath as his phone rang and rang.

"Hello?"

It was Mrs. Shaw. I hung up fast.

In bed that night I daydreamed that I met Craddoc in the commons before first period and he put his arm around me and said, "Know a secluded little place where we can have a talk?"

It didn't happen like that. I saw Craddoc in the commons before first period. He was standing with a group of his friends. He saw me and said nothing.

Maggot Head

The whole week was a drag. I avoided the commons, so at least I wouldn't see Craddoc ignoring me. On Saturday I baby-sat for Dad and paid Robyn her money back. On Sunday I washed my sweaters and stretched them on newspapers, wandered around the house, and finally took off for Jenny's.

Mrs. Sawyer opened the front door. "Come on in, Elsie. They've all gone to a movie, but I expect them home soon."

I backed away. "That's O.K. I'll . . ."

"No, come on in and have some tea with me. I could use the company."

She brought the tea tray into the living room and set it on the coffee table. "I wanted to stay home to wash my

hair. I did and I was starting to get bored when you arrived. Sugar or lemon?"

"Lemon, thanks."

She settled back in her chair. "How've you been? How's
that handsome football player of yours?"

I sipped the tea. "Handsome, but I don't think he's mine
any more."

"Why is that?"

"I got jealous because he didn't pay any attention to me
at the Halloween party, so I went home, and when he
called, I hung up."

She looked thoughtfully at me over her teacup. "Elsie,
do you think a popular, handsome football player would
really like you?"

"I guess not."

"And did you expect him to get bored with you and go
off with a popular, prettier girl?"

"I guess so."

"Have another cookie."

I looked at the plate and shook my head. "I don't need
to stuff myself with cookies."

She got up and helped herself to one. "I remember you
were a sad, fat little girl when you first came to help Jenny
with her fractions."

"I guess I'm just the same, except not fat."

"Maybe even still fat on the inside?"

"Meaning what?" I hadn't meant my voice to sound so
sharp.

Mrs. Sawyer held up a hand. "Wait a minute. I didn't mean fatheaded, for Heaven's sake. What I meant was maybe you don't think of yourself as lovable even if you are thin."

"Oh." I began wishing Jenny would hurry up.

She put her cup on the table beside her and leaned forward. "I surely don't want to hurt your feelings, Elsie. The point I'm trying to make is sometimes what we expect we make come true. And you said you expected to lose your boyfriend."

I took up a cookie, calories or not, and bit into it. There was the sound of a car door slamming and Kenny's feet pounding up the front steps. He burst in the door, followed by his dad and Jenny. "You should have come, Mom. It was the neatest show."

She held up her hand. "Spare me the details."

"Dinner about ready?" Mr. Sawyer asked, shaking out his wet raincoat.

"No, it isn't." There was a bite to Mrs. Sawyer's tone that left me holding my cookie in midair.

Mr. Sawyer frowned. "It's five-twenty. What were you planning?"

"I wasn't planning anything. I thought I deserved one afternoon off a week, since you take two."

I stood up, mumbled that I better go, and headed for the back door. Jenny pulled on my arm in the hall. "Come on in my room. We can't hear them over the stereo."

I came, a little nervously. I'd never heard her parents

fight before. She cranked the stereo up.

"What have you and Mom been doing?" Jenny asked me when we were stretched out on her bed listening to the Go-Go's.

"Playing Psychiatric Hospital, I think."

"Oh, Mom loves that. Did she tell you how to do affirmations?"

"No."

"No? Well, maybe she saves those for the second session." Jenny rolled over on her stomach. "Heard from Craddoc?"

"No," I said. "And I don't think I will. Jack been around?"

"When he hasn't got anything else to do."

I nodded. They were both my friends, but I couldn't see Jenny understanding what Jack was about or Jack flying on the ground for Jenny.

"I always thought Jack liked you," Jenny said. "Remember when he took you to Sharon's party in eighth grade and spiked the punch and then drank half of it himself? Mrs. Hinkler drove us all home, and you put your arm around Jack to keep his head up and then insisted he get off at your place, and you got out of the car still holding him until you could push him behind some bushes to puke. I looked out the back window and saw his red head bobbing up and down through the leaves. That was so funny. All the way to my house Mrs. Hinkler kept telling Sharon that she thought you were a very forward girl and she didn't see why you were invited to our parties."

I rested my head on my chin, remembering that night. And remembering Jack kissing me in the kitchen when he was just a little drunk.

Jenny got up to put on another record. "How did you ever get him home from your house?"

"It wasn't easy."

She laughed. "He was so embarrassed the next day. He never asked you to go to a party with him again, did he?"

He did once, but it was a night I couldn't go and maybe he thought I didn't want to. That's the one thing Jack and I never got straight.

I pulled myself up and reached for my jacket.

"Listen," Jenny said, "do you remember any of your algebra? You're so good in math and I'm so lousy. Do you think you could help me a bit before you split?"

I thought so and I did.

The next Saturday I took my math and English over to Dad's so I could study while the baby slept. First, I cleaned up the messy living room, though, because I don't like working in the middle of a pig pen. The baby made tiny noises at nine o'clock. I got him up, changed and fed him, and then, instead of putting him down, I set his bottle on the floor, wrapped his soft, blue blanket around him, cuddled his sleepy, warm little body against my shoulder, and rocked away.

I'm going to have five children when I get married. There's going to be big, steaming Thanksgiving dinners, birthday parties with streamers and candles and cake and ice cream, and I'll have a huge Christmas tree, and the children won't be able to get out of bed Christmas morning until the tree is lit and the house is warm, and they'll squeal when they see the mounds of presents under the tree. Craddoc would make a good daddy, firm and kind and fair.

I thought about that. He should listen to me if I say I'm sorry. Hello, Craddoc, I'm sorry. That's O.K., Elsie, good-bye. How did his mother maneuver me smooth as cream? Hello, Craddoc, I called to tell you two things: first, I'm sorry I was jealous, and second, will you go out to dinner with me on Sunday?

Not dinner. That costs too much. A movie and the A and W. I put the baby in his crib and sorted through the pile of newspapers for the theater section. It had to be a show that was funny and tender so Craddoc would get in the right mood. There was a rerun of *E.T.* at the Edmonds Theater. *Ab*-solutely perfect!

I dialed his number before I got too chicken. What if they were all asleep? He was probably out having a ball.

"Hello." It was Craddoc.

"Hello," I said, scrinching up my shoulders. "This is Elsie. I called to tell you two things. First, I'm sorry I got jealous and acted bitchy, and second, I wondered if you could pick me up about seven o'clock tomorrow evening so I could take you to a show and buy you a root beer float at the A and W?"

"What did you do? Rob a bank?"

"No, I've been baby-sitting for my dad. That's what I'm doing now. Uh . . . have you seen *E.T.*?"

"Twice."

"How about a third time?"

"O.K."

"I'll see you at seven o'clock tomorrow, then. Good-bye." I put the phone down and whirled around the living room. It worked! Smooth as cream!

Sunday morning I washed my hair, went totally through every outfit I had, and decided on jeans and my blue angora sweater. Casual, soft, and sexy. Perfect! About a quarter to seven I threw my rain jacket over a living room chair and sat down to watch TV with Mama and Robyn.

At seven on the dot, the doorbell rang. Robyn jumped up to answer it. After she let Craddoc in, she passed by the back of my chair, muttering, "How'd you work that?"

Mama invited Craddoc to sit down, but I told her we had to make a show and we'd be back home about ten-thirty.

Even though it was a rerun, there was a long line at the theater. I bought popcorn at the stand next to the ticket window and brought it back to Craddoc. He took the box I handed him with one eyebrow raised. "A big-time spender, huh?"

"Craddoc," I said as I munched away, "do your folks have a big Thanksgiving?"

"Grandmas and cousins and turkey and dressing and pumpkin pies."

"I thought you were the only grandchild?"

"On my father's side. My mother's sister has six kids."

I sighed. "That must be neat. We take my grandmother out to dinner in a restaurant and listen to her complain about her bad back."

"Come to my house," Craddoc said.

"Oh, no. I was just dreaming about having a big Thanksgiving when I have a family."

"Have it now, too. I'll have my mom call you."

"No, Craddoc, don't. I didn't mean that."

"Listen, Elsie." He wiped his buttery hand on his jeans before he took me by the arm and said sternly, "You've got to stop thinking nobody wants you around and start thinking they're glad to have you."

"That's easy for you to say when you're the big football player."

He dropped my arm. "Oh, come off it. I'm Craddoc, just Craddoc. Like you're just Elsie. This isn't going to work, you know, unless you get your head straight."

Fear slipped around my insides. Watch your expectations, maggot head, I told myself.

Craddoc didn't talk to me again until we were sitting in our theater seats waiting for the movie to start. "Do you like being miserable?" he said.

I looked at him, surprised. "No."

"I don't like being miserable, either, and you made me miserable the last two weeks."

"You could have said something to me in the commons."

"Why should I? So you could do it all again?"

"I won't do it again, Craddoc. I promise." I slunk down in my seat as the movie came on and was very relieved to hear Craddoc's burst of laughter at the big brother's expression when the little brother showed him E.T.

Craddoc was in a great mood at the end of the film. He held my hand going out of the theater and rapped away about extraterrestrials while driving to the A and W. "You know," he told me as we waited for our order, "maybe it's lucky I've got you so young so I can train you. What I should do is put a thick collar around your neck—"

"Thick collar!"

"Right. And put a leash on it, and every time I talk to a girl and see your blue eyes turn green, I'll yank the collar."

"Craddoc!" I punched him in the arm, and he grabbed my wrist. "Craddoc, why don't you just buy a cattle prod?"

"Now there's an idea. Let's see. Which place will I prod you?"

I punched him with my other fist, and he grabbed that wrist, too. "Craddoc, that isn't nice."

"How do you know it isn't nice?" He held my wrists wide apart until my arms were spread out like bird's wings.

"Craddoc! This isn't comfortable."

"How about this, then." He dropped my hands and slipped his arms around me and pulled me tight against him.

The girl with the root beer floats said, "Uh, I hate to bother you, but . . ."

Look at the Mess You Made

Monday morning Craddoc walked me to first period. I was bouncing along to the tune in my head, so he asked me what I was humming.

"It's a song we're doing in choir." I smiled up at him and sang, "Isn't this a ha-ppy daay?"

He laughed and we went the rest of the way to home ec with our arms around each other.

I was barely in my seat, giving Jenny the details about getting Craddoc back, when Sharon pranced over to our end of the sewing room. "Did Katie dump Craddoc already? I saw her in the commons this morning with somebody else."

"We wouldn't know," Jenny told her.

"She's such a darling girl." Sharon sighed. "It doesn't surprise me that all the guys like her."

"It doesn't surprise us, either," Jenny said. "You'd better get in your seat. The bell's about to ring."

I watched Sharon go back to her table. "Do you think he went out with Katie Bentler?"

"What does it matter? You've got him."

I eyed Jenny closely. "Do you know something I don't know?"

"Nope. I don't know anything. Don't hassle every little thing, Elsie."

"It isn't a little thing. He gave me a big line about how miserable I'd made him for two weeks."

"So? You probably did."

We had to shut up while Mrs. Ash took the roll. I figured I'd find out from Jack after English class, anyway.

Jack came into English class fifteen minutes late and handed Miss Bickford another note. I could see she didn't like it, but she took the note and let him sit down. He looked pleased with himself.

"What was it this time?" I asked him on the way out.

"It's my new system."

"What new system?" We were weaving in and out of the between-classes crowd, and my books got knocked out of my arm. Jack helped me pick them up.

"About this system?" I asked when we were on our way again.

"Easy. Anytime I need to be late, I go sit in the chairs

outside the counselor's office. When she calls me in, I ask about my credits or how to get an after-school job, and when she finishes telling me she gives me a pass to class."

"O.K., but why do you need to be late?"

"In case I want to stop by the woods awhile."

"The woods?"

"Ya, the woods. You know, the woods in back of the auto shop."

"Jack, you're going to get caught."

"No way."

"Yes, you will. Some teacher will see you coming or going."

"No. No. Kids come and go in the woods all day."

We were near the chorus room, and I was more interested in pumping Jack about Craddoc than arguing about the woods, so I grabbed his arm and held him by the door. "Jack, what did Craddoc do on weekends while we were split up?"

"Played pool with Kevin and me over at my house."

"Did he take out Katie Bentler?"

"I told you. Craddoc doesn't like stupid women."

I let go of his arm. Before he took off, he gave me a look that let me know I wasn't too bright, either.

Mama went out Friday night, so I had to stay in with Robyn and miss the next football game. Craddoc came over Saturday after dinner and invited me to a party that night at Jamison's. While we waited for Mama to come home, he sat at the kitchen table and gave me a play-by-play

73

account of the game, or tried to, over the noise of Cecile and Robyn playing video games in the living room. It was a relief when they turned off the TV and went into Robyn's room.

I had just gotten Craddoc a Coke when I heard the front door open and, "Elsie, get in here!"

"Excuse me," I said to Craddoc, and hurried into the living room.

She was standing in the middle of the floor with her hands on her hips, staring at Robyn's Atari games, tablet, pencils, and empty Coke cans, which were strewn around the floor. "What is this mess?"

"Well, Robyn . . ."

"Don't 'well, Robyn' me. I don't appreciate coming home to a garbage dump after I leave you in charge. Now get your butt in gear!"

She stalked into the kitchen, and I heard her say, "Craddoc, I didn't know you were here."

I gathered up Robyn's junk, took it into her room, and dumped it in her lap while saying every four-letter word I knew. When I was finished, I went back in the kitchen, knowing I'd have to tell Craddoc to forget about Jamison's party.

"You about ready to go?" He flipped his empty Coke can into the garbage bag under the sink.

"No, I don't think . . ." I glanced nervously at Mama, who was leaning against the end of the counter sipping a drink.

74

"I told Bette I'd have you home by twelve. You going in those clothes?"

"No. Oh, no. I'll just be a minute." How did he do that? Bette?

"How did you do that?" I asked him as we drove to Jamison's. "And when did you start calling her Bette?"

"She told me to." He flashed me a grin. "It's the Shaw charm."

I thought of several replies, but kept my mouth shut. I wasn't going to blow this party.

And I didn't blow the party. I didn't have a prime time, because I'm not the greatest mixer, but I smiled a lot and danced some and kept my attention away from Katie Bentler, who, fortunately for me, was concentrating on the halfback. About eleven o'clock Craddoc gathered me up, told Jamison he had to get Cinderella home, and headed me out to the car. Some kids, sitting in the car parked behind Craddoc's, were passing around a party bowl and, just as we went by, one of them opened the car door, which lit the dome light, and I saw Katie Bentler in the back seat. Craddoc waved to her, but didn't make any comment to me. I grinned all the way to our secluded spot, thinking what a ball it would be to **tell** Sharon about her darling cheerleader. I couldn't, though. Sharon's mouth is too big.

Craddoc's secluded spot for the night was the road below the oil docks that ended overlooking the sound. He pulled up, turned off the car, and settled me against his shoulder. We sat together, silently watching the water until I turned my head to look up at him, wondering what he was thinking about. It was my mother.

"How come you call her Mama? Most kids don't do that after they're six."

"It *is* kind of babyish," I agreed. "We just never changed to Mom, I guess."

"Are you afraid of her?"

"Sure."

"What can she do to you?"

"She could have made me stay home tonight, for instance. And she would have if you hadn't gotten to her."

"All I did was tell her she looked a little beat and give her some sympathy." Craddoc drummed on the steering wheel. "Do you hate her?"

"I suppose I do."

"Why's that?"

A montage of scenes flooded my head. Me standing by her chair while she fed the baby, hoping she'd read me a story, talk to me, pat my head. Me watching her and Robyn go off in the car together, crying because she said I was old enough to be left home alone. Me waddling behind her, knowing she didn't want people to think I belonged to her.

Craddoc jiggled me with his shoulder. "You spacing out?"

"No, I was just thinking. I guess I hate her because those years I was fat I knew she was ashamed of me. And

76

that does something to your head. To know your mother wishes she could get rid of you. And what really makes me hate her is if she'd given me any attention when I was little I wouldn't have consoled myself with food and would never have ended up looking like the circus fat lady."

"Your old man taking off must have really messed her head." He smiled to himself. "He was crazy. She's one attractive lady."

I sat up straight. "What time is it?"

"Time for a kiss."

"No, Craddoc." I pulled away from him by leaning over for my purse. I tipped the visor mirror so I could see a darkened reflection of my face and concentrated on combing my hair. Craddoc sat back in his seat and watched me.

I put my comb away. "We better get going. It must be nearly twelve."

"I don't think so," Craddoc said. "I don't think we'll go until we talk a little more."

Beneath my burn, I had just enough sense to keep telling myself, Keep your mouth shut, Elsie, keep your mouth shut.

"I can see her side of it," he said slowly. "She's got a rough go of it, trying to make it by herself in the real estate business. She must work twelve hours a day."

"Good for you." It came out through clenched teeth. "Before Dad remarried and reduced the support payments, she *played* twelve hours a day."

"And"—he took hold of my hand—"I can see yours." I tugged on my hand, but he held it tight. "There must have been some reason to treat you the way she did. And she treats you shitty now, for that matter."

Tears started in my eyes and I blinked fast. I was *not* going to cry.

He reached up and stroked my face. I stiffened, but he kept running his fingers lightly over my cheek. "Elsie, your mother's good-lookin' and so are you . . . and you're smart and sensitive and . . . hurt and . . ." He bent down and kissed my damp eyes. "And I love you."

Tears streamed down my face, and I fumbled in my purse for a tissue.

"I tell you I love you for the first time, and you cry?"

"It isn't just your first time. It's the first time anybody has said that to me."

He gathered me in his arms and held me while I sniffled and dabbed at my eyes. "I was trying to get you to see her side of it, too."

"I know she has her side of it, Craddoc, but it doesn't do any good when she humiliates me in front of my friends. I can't watch Robyn all the time. I can't even figure out what will set her off. Whenever she's pissed, I'm her target."

"You know, you could learn to handle her."

"That's easy for yo-ou to say. You have a nice family who do-otes on you." I got the words out over my hic-

cups. "I have enough trou-ble keeping it together."
"I could scare you and make those hiccups go away."
"No, Cra-Craddoc," I said. "Just hold me tight."
And he did.

Honey Bear

Mrs. Shaw called a couple of nights before Thanksgiving. I had her hold the phone while I went into the kitchen and interrupted Mama and Robyn's checker game. "Mrs. Shaw wants to know if I can come for Thanksgiving dinner."

"Oh, no!" Robyn said. "Go to dinner with us." Mama kept her eyes on the checkerboard, and Robyn watched her. "Say no, Mama."

"Mrs. Shaw is waiting," I said.

Mama shrugged, the way she does. "If that's what you want to do . . ."

"Oh, crap!" Robyn slammed a handful of checkers on the table.

"I thought you hated me," I told her before I went back to the phone.

Thanksgiving at the Shaws' beat dinner out with my family. The huge table was set with crystal, flowers, papier mâché turkeys standing above a sprinkling of candy corn, cranberry sauce, pickles, olives. . . . The one grandma wasn't there because she was in the hospital, and that part was sad, but the rest was a ball. The cousins whooped when Craddoc refused a glass of champagne because he was in training, and they kept up a running gag all evening on the perils of Super Straight bedding down with his barbell.

I helped Mrs. Shaw clear the table, and as we filled the dishwasher, I told her I loved big family celebrations and hoped I'd have lots of kids someday. She said she'd wanted five, but couldn't have any more after the first one. She hoped she'd have a house full of grandchildren.

I hugged Craddoc tight before I got out of the car to go up to my door.

"Hmmm," he said, pulling down my coat collar to kiss my neck. "If this is what I get, I'll bring you home every Thanksgiving."

On Friday morning I promised Jenny I'd help her with her algebra before we went Christmas shopping in the Alderwood Mall. I bumped into Kenny going up the Sawyers' steps—or Kenny bumped into me. He was racing around from the neighbor's backyard, yelling his head off at somebody behind him. "Poopy pee legs! Poopy pee legs, poopy pee legs!"

The kid who was after him came barreling around the corner, but screeched to a halt when he saw me. He stood at the edge of the yard making faces at Kenny. Kenny smirked back at the kid and taunted him one last time, "Poopy pee legs!"

Jenny met us at the door. "What's going on out there?"

"None of your business," Kenny told her.

Jenny had her homework spread out on the dining room table, and while she practiced an equation I had taught her, I thought about Kenny. "How does Kenny get along with other kids?" I asked her after she finished one section in the algebra book.

"Sometimes O.K. Sometimes not. He argues with them too much."

"He's too honest. You have to be a politician to be really popular." I gave out a short laugh. "Like Diane."

Jenny raised her eyebrows. "Or Craddoc."

"Yeah, Craddoc would make the perfect diplomat. Always there with the right touch. *Or* the right explanation," I added, flashing on how he'd twisted getting off on my mother into "helping" me understand her. I pulled Jenny's book forward. "Let's get this junk finished so we can split."

Jenny was working away again when Kenny came in and stood by my chair. "Elsie, do mother rats eat their babies?"

"I don't know. I think the male rat might. Maybe you better put him in a separate cage."

"I have him in a separate cage. With some of the others."

"Others?"

Jenny looked up. "His first baby rats have had baby rats."

Kenny ignored his sister. "Elsie, last night I counted the new babies and there were six. Now there are only three.

"Have you got an encyclopedia?"

"No. Mom bought me one book on raising small animals. It just says how to feed the rats and that you can sell them to the pet shops."

"The snakes would be delighted," Jenny said.

He turned on her. "Nobody's talking to you."

"Yes, they are." She shuffled her papers into her Pee Chee. "I'm finished and we're leaving. And you better get over to Raymond's house because I'm locking the doors while we're gone."

"I'm not going to Raymond's."

"You are, too. Mom called his mother and made arrangements last night. I get one day by myself over Thanksgiving vacation."

"I'm not going."

Jenny's face was swelling with anger. "Listen, you're not going to spoil . . ."

"Wait a minute," I interrupted. "Have you got any money, Kenny?"

"I've got my birthday money."

"Good. You can spend it today. Give me Raymond's phone number, Jenny, and we'll leave them at the movies while we shop."

Kenny followed Jenny and me to the phone. "It's not going to work. Raymond won't go with me."

"Yes, he will." When Raymond's mother answered the phone, I asked politely for Raymond and smiled at Kenny while I waited. "Raymond? This is Elsie, Kenny's sister's friend. We're going to Alderwood Mall this afternoon and Kenny would very much like to take you to the movie theater. Will you ask your mother if you can go? Tell her we'll take good care of you."

I confirmed all the plans with Raymond's mother and when I hung up Kenny said, "He'll go?"

"Sure. It's my new system."

"Smoooth," Jenny said.

"It should be. I learned it from Craddoc's mother."

Raymond turned out to be a pain. Jenny had to hold his hand getting on the metro bus, and as soon as he was on, he began whining that he had to go to the toilet. I told him jokes to make him forget about it, and every time he laughed he hung on to the crotch of his pants. We rushed him across the mall to the theater so he could use the lavatory, but when Kenny finished paying for the tickets Raymond headed for the concession stand and insisted on waiting in line to buy himself a candy bar before he went in. He held his candy bar with one hand and his pants with the other as he and Kenny disappeared into the theater. Poopy pee legs was a prime name for him.

The Salvation Army lady was ringing her bell outside the Bon Marché so I put my change in her bucket as Jenny and I went by. We trailed in and out of the shops and Jenny rapped away about both our birthdays coming up in December and mine being only eight days away. I tried to distract her by pointing out the clothes in the store windows, but most were party dresses.

"I think *I'll* have a party," she decided. "What are you going to do?"

"Nothing, probably. We don't celebrate birthdays much."

"You have cake and ice cream, don't you?"

"If Mama remembers."

"What do you mean, if your mother remembers?" We had reached Ernst by then and went in to check out the toys. "How could she forget? I make out a list, don't you?"

"No, Mama thinks presents should be a surprise."

"Forgetting would be some surprise." Jenny zeroed in on a display of robots.

I propped myself up against the counter while she set each robot in motion, and I remembered back four years to the birthday Mama forgot. It was more like a shock than a surprise. A sickening shock: watching Mama light a cigarette at the end of dinner and slowly realizing she was not going to get up for cake and candles. I hadn't seen a cake among the groceries she brought home. I thought maybe she'd left it in the car on purpose till dinner was over.

Robyn pulled out the present she'd had hidden in her lap. "Happy birthday, Elsie."

Mama put her cigarette in the ashtray. "Oh, my God, it *is* your birthday. I forgot all about it."

Robyn stared at Mama. "You forgot!?" Then she turned to me with such pity on her face my fingers trembled as I undid her package.

"What a neat bracelet." I slipped it over my hand and held out my arm for Robyn to admire.

"It's real copper. I'll do the dishes since it's your birthday." She got up from the table and I got up, too. I wanted to get to my bedroom, fast.

Mama pushed her chair back. "I'll tell you what. I'll take you to a show to celebrate."

"No, that's O.K." I headed out of the kitchen.

"Come on, Elsie," Robyn called after me. "It'll be fun."

"No, I have too much homework." I got out of there before they could see me cry.

"Come on, Space." Jenny was holding a large silver robot. "Let's go find a saleslady. Kenny will get off on this one."

Jenny bought the robot, which took most of her money, and I bought cassettes for Robyn, which took most of mine. We spent the rest of the afternoon munchin' down at Baskin Robbins until the movie was out. To my relief, she didn't mention birthdays again.

By the time Saturday came around I had myself so carefully coached to feel no emotion I didn't care one way or another when Mama came home early and said she'd make dinner. I went on into my bedroom to study. I looked up from my books once when it seemed there was a lot of opening and closing of doors, but I didn't hear anything else unusual, so I went back to my social studies paper. At six o'clock Robyn opened my door, her dark eyes shining with excitement. "Dinner's ready."

I'd been her age the year Mama forgot my birthday. It would matter then, but not at fifteen. I washed my hands in the bathroom and went down the hall to the kitchen.

"Happy birthday!!" they all screamed. Robyn and Jack and Jenny and Craddoc. I stood in the doorway, stunned.

Craddoc got up from the table. "You'll have to have my present first because I couldn't wrap her up." He reached into a carton by the back door and lifted out a honey-colored puppy.

"Ohhh." I cuddled the soft, furry thing in my arms.

"It's a thoroughbred chow," Craddoc told me proudly, and turned to Mama. "The female chow housebreaks her puppies, Bette, and chows have no dog odor."

"That's handy." She stood over against the stove. I was relieved to see she was smiling.

"Let's eat," Robyn said. "Let's eat."

Mama served spaghetti and salad and hot French bread. While the others porked down, I picked bits of meat off my plate and fed them to the puppy in my lap.

87

HOW DO YOU LOSE THOSE NINTH GRADE BLUES?

"They're one-man dogs." Craddoc passed around more bread. "You can't give them away after they're grown because they won't attach to a new owner."

"Who would want to?" Jenny said.

"Not me," I muttered, and to my embarrassment tears slid down my cheeks. I bent my head to hide them, and my puppy stretched up and licked my face with a black tongue.

"Fine thing," Jack said. "What are you going to do when you open *our* presents?"

"It's only because I'm happy," I tried to explain. "She looks like a little bear. A honey bear. I'll call her Honey Bear."

Mama brought out the cake, and we ate it with ice cream on top, then I started in on the pile of packages. Jenny gave me Oscar de la Renta perfume, which I love. Robyn's present amazed me. "Oh, whoa, a book on computer programming. How did you think that up?"

"Well"—she pinked with pleasure—"I know you like math."

Jack's present was dangling blue earrings.

"Who helped you pick those out?" Jenny asked him.

"Me," he said. "I know what looks good on Elsie."

I swished my head back and forth after I had the earrings on.

"He sure does know what looks good on you," Craddoc admitted.

"Now," Robyn ordered, "open the big present."

88

The "big present" was an expensive-looking gray-blue tweed blazer. "Try it on and see if it fits," Mama said.

"That's sharp, Bette," Craddoc told her when I modeled the jacket.

I stroked a wool sleeve in appreciation. "Thank you. It's lovely." I suppose I was expected to kiss her, but I couldn't have managed that.

Jack tipped his chair back from the table. "Now that you have the loot, what do we do next?"

"I've got a new video game that four can play," Robyn offered.

"One, two, three, four, five, six," Jack counted.

"Mama and I will do the dishes and you guys play." Robyn lifted the cake plate off the table.

"You're all right."

"Only on birthdays," Robyn told him.

"Come to think of it, you've been nice a few times lately when it wasn't my birthday," I said.

Robyn pretended she didn't hear me.

Craddoc, Jack, and Jenny played the video game. I sat in the rocker and patted Honey Bear while she slept against my shoulder.

Girls Always Scream Twice

Registration for second semester began in December. The counselors came into the English classes to help the ninth graders with schedules and four-year plans. The first side of the ditto that our counselor passed out contained blanks for our list of courses, and the back side contained blanks for our statements on our goals, strengths, weaknesses, and what we did "for fun."

Our counselor talked to us about graduation requirements and building up a strong academic background for success in college. I wrote biology, chemistry, college prep comp, and Spanish 1 to 6 on my paper. The Spanish teacher has a reputation as a human being, and I figured I could use one of those.

The counselor put the math sequence on the blackboard, and I copied down math analysis, computer programming, algebra 3 and 4, and calculus. I added three years of neophonics instead of choir because I was singing two solos in the Christmas concert and I thought I'd be chosen for the advanced group.

Jack shook his head at my selection of classes, and I shook my head at what he wrote down under fun: "I like to party harty, play sports, and go to concerts. I also like cruisen with my friends."

"It's the truth," he said.

"I don't figure you to last the year," I said, which, unfortunately, was also the truth.

Jack got away with putting dry ice in the toilets (the janitor lost it), setting firecrackers off in assembly (the two vice principals and the principal converged on the freshman section, but there are three hundred and fifteen of us), and hiding a stink bomb in the commons (we booked out of that place six seconds faster than for a fire drill).

Jack's luck began to run out when his system broke down. Jenny and I first heard about it from Sharon. She came breathlessly into home ec with the news that she'd seen Jack heading for the counselor's office with Mr. Swenson, the shop teacher.

"So what?" Jenny said. "Maybe they wanted to talk to her about Jack's program."

"No way," Sharon said. "Swenson was boiling."

Jenny walked down to the English room with me so we

could get the story from Jack. He made like it was no big thing. "Oh, Swenson hollered at the counselor for giving me so many passes. He told her she should be able to see I was pulling the wool over her eyes, and if I was ever late to class again, he was kicking me out."

"What did the counselor do?" Jenny asked.

"She just sat there and took it. Swenson's an ass."

We didn't hear about Jack's suspension until three days after it happened. Jenny had invited me over to her house for Saturday night. I was uneasy about going because Honey Bear sleeps beside *my* bed and Jenny's cat, D.D., sleeps on *her* bed.

"No problem," Jenny told me. "Since D.D.'s been spayed, she acts like she's sixty."

Mrs. Sawyer was on her way out to shop when I arrived. "She's darling," she said when she saw Honey Bear, "but is she housebroken?"

"Completely," I said. "The mother dog does that when the puppies are six weeks old."

"Hmmm, I wish she'd given me lessons." Mrs. Sawyer left, and Kenny and his dad went bowling.

Jenny called Jack and asked him over and suggested he bring Craddoc along. Jack couldn't. He was grounded because Piker had suspended him for a week after he caught him in the woods.

I rolled over and sat up on the floor where I'd been playing on my back with Honey Bear. "I told him he was going to get caught! He hasn't been straight in English more than ten days out of a month. I wondered why he wasn't in class Thursday or Friday. Didn't you notice?"

"I don't always see Jack," Jenny said. "He has lots of friends, you know."

I knew.

Jenny and I spent the afternoon making up dough for Christmas ornaments and baking them in the oven. She didn't seem bothered by Jack's problems, but they bothered me. I'd liked Jack ever since the fifth grade when I'd busted him in the mouth with a baseball bat and he'd never told anyone it was me who'd split his lip. There was a kind of special nonverbal communication between us. I had to explain my feelings to Craddoc, but not to Jack. Like the earrings—Jack knew what went with me.

Kenny and his dad came home about five o'clock with a big bucket of Kentucky Fried Chicken. Mrs. Sawyer arrived five minutes later. She was flyin'.

"Wait till you see your ravishing wife in her new outfits," she told her husband.

Kenny looked over the packages she'd plunked down on the dining room table. "Didn't you buy us anything?"

"Yes, but you can't see yours until Christmas." She took a raspberry cashmere sweater out of the first box and held it up to her neck. "What do you think?"

"Great," Mr. Sawyer said. "But maybe we better eat before you model. This stuff will get cold."

"Jenny can set the table. I want to show you one more thing."

Jenny put around the plates and I put out the silver-ware while Mrs. Sawyer tried on a leather jacket with a fox fur collar. She twirled around the table. "What do you think?"

"Uh, nice," Mr. Sawyer said, opening the chicken bucket.

Jenny was eyeing her mother intently. "Let me try it on."

Her mother handed over the jacket and sat down at the table with a happy sigh. "I forgot to eat lunch. I'm famished."

"What do you think, Daddy?" Wearing the jacket, Jenny turned her back on us and arched her head over her shoulder toward her dad.

His face burst into a big smile. "Pretty cute."

"Mother?" Jenny did another turn.

Mrs. Sawyer looked up from the chicken leg she was eating and licked a finger. "Cute, but a little old for you."

"Oh, I don't know," Mr. Sawyer said. "I think it looks better on Jenny than it does on you."

The radiance drained from Mrs. Sawyer's face. It was true the jacket looked better on Jenny, but I sickened as I watched Jenny's mother try to eat another bite of chicken and then drop the piece of meat back on her plate. "Well, if you really think so . . ." she said slowly.

Jenny pulled the collar around her face until just her brown eyes showed through the fur. "Why don't you give it to me for my birthday? Huh, Daddy?"

94

Mr. Sawyer nodded his approval. "That's a good solution," he said.

"You can have it now," Mrs. Sawyer said quietly.

"Really?? *Awe*-some!!" Jenny bounced from the room to admire herself in her bedroom mirror. I concentrated on watching Kenny stir the gravy into his mashed potatoes and didn't look up until I felt Mr. Sawyer become aware of his wife's silence.

"You can buy yourself another jacket next Saturday," he suggested.

"I have to work next Saturday."

"Seems like you're working a lot of overtime."

"Yes," she said. "Seems like."

I didn't say anything to Jenny about how bad the whole scene made me feel. We lay on her bed after dinner, listening to her stereo, and phrases went through my head that I would have liked to have said. "You don't know how lucky you are to have a mother that neat." "Even if she is too short to look good in the jacket, you could have waited till she figured that out." "You spoiled the whole day for her."

It was all too dumb to say. Especially since I knew Jenny had just set up the best birthday I ever had.

I was relieved when we went to bed. I had succeeded in fighting off my downer by cuddling Honey Bear and was falling asleep when Jack's five-day suspension registered in my mind. How many total days would that make Jack absent in English? I promised myself I'd call him and tell him I'd help him with the final essay on *Great Expectqtions* so he'd have a good paper to bring to class when he returned. That let me finally fall asleep.

In the middle of the night Jenny slipped out of bed, and I figured she must be getting up to go to the toilet. I drifted off again, but was startled wide awake by two piercing screams. I threw the covers off and ran to the bathroom. There was Jenny backed up against the wall, pointing at a big black-and-white rat which was teetering on the edge of the toilet, trying to get a drink of water out of the toilet bowl.

Jenny moved out behind me and headed for Kenny's room. "Kenny, you get out of bed and get your rat. Get up right now and get your rat."

Kenny came padding down the hall and picked up the rat. "You don't have to scream so much," he said to Jenny, who was following him. "It's just the daddy rat."

"Well, what's the 'daddy rat' doing in the toilet?"

Kenny didn't answer her. He took his rat into his bedroom and came back to the bathroom with a shallow dish. He filled the dish with water, carried it out the door, and bumped into Mrs. Sawyer, who was coming down the hall.

She brushed the water from her sopping gown. "For Heaven's sake, Kenny, *what* is going on?"

"Kenny's rat was in the toilet when I got up to go to the bathroom," Jenny told her mother.

"He was just a little thirsty, that's all," Kenny said.

"Well, why don't you remember to give it water if you're

going to keep it?" Jenny yelled after him.

"Jenny, really, that's enough screaming." Mrs. Sawyer came into the bathroom and tried to blot the water from her nightgown with a towel.

"Just how would you like to get up and go to the bathroom when you're half asleep and find a rat in the toilet?" Jenny asked her, joining us in the bathroom.

A picture of that flashed in my head, and I let out a giggle.

"It's not funny, Elsie." Jenny plopped herself down on the toilet and began to pee. "Mother, every time I bring guests here the whole house smells of rats. It's humiliating to have your house stink. He doesn't even give them water or clean the cages. Why do you let him keep them?"

Mrs. Sawyer gave up on the blotting and put the towel back on the rack. "He has to have something to play with."

"Then why don't you buy him a bike like other kids?" Jenny got off the toilet and I got on, and Mrs. Sawyer went to find herself a dry nightgown.

Back in bed, Jenny said, "Couldn't you see us getting to have rats when we were seven?"

I couldn't.

No-Credit Situation

I left Jenny's about three Sunday afternoon. There was plenty of time before dinner, so I decided to walk Honey Bear over to Jack's house. I'm very careful about keeping promises, to myself or anybody else. I'll say this for my mother, she never lies. My dad does. He'll tell any story to get himself off the hook. I hate that, and I avoid conversations with people who lie. What's the point?

I had to climb Jack's steps slowly, waiting for Honey Bear to hop up each one. Jack's dad let me in and showed me where the rec room was. Jack and his older brother were playing a game of pool.

His brother straightened up from the table when he saw me. "You didn't tell me about the blonde."

"I have to keep her hidden," Jack said. "She belongs to Craddoc, and he's bigger than I am. Elsie, this is Kevin."

"Hello, Kevin," I said.

"Well, hello, Elsie! You just sit down with your doggie and we'll finish up this game quick." It was evidently Kevin's turn, and he cleared the table with one shot like I'd seen Craddoc do.

Jack took another cue off the rack. "Come on and play, Elsie."

"I don't know how."

Kevin walked over to the couch and took me by the hand. "We'll have that little problem solved in no time."

And he did. It was fun. Even the part where Kevin wrapped his arms around me every time he helped me position the cue.

"Your brother's some operator," I said to Jack after Kevin's friends came and took him away.

"He likes to think he is." Jack got us Cokes from the rec room bar, and we sat down to drink them.

"What I really came over for was to help you do your English essay."

"Duh."

"No, Jack. You're liable to have ten absences and tardies by the time you get back, and then Bickford can say you get no credit in her class. That's a whole semester wasted."

"Most of the tardies are excused."

"It's excused *or* unexcused. The only thing is, you can

make up the excused ones, but you haven't made up any. So you better have a good essay ready to impress her with. It's due Monday."

Jack put his Coke can on the floor and tried to pet Honey Bear, but she backed away. "Craddoc wasn't kidding about her being a one-man dog."

"I know."

"The thing is, Elsie, the class is such a waste of time."

"True, but you have to have English if you're going to graduate."

Jack leaned against the pillows and let out a long sigh. "I'm trying to figure out if it's worth it."

He had me there. Jack is smart, but he doesn't get into subjects like music and math the way I do. He likes to read, and he might enjoy English if enjoy were possible.

I sat and Jack sat. Finally he said, "Oh, well, let's give it a try."

I was doing my essay on the character and motivation of Miss Havisham, so we did Jack's on the convict. We were about finished with the rough draft when I heard Craddoc's voice. He came loping down the basement stairs a few minutes later. "Oh, oh. There's something you two haven't told me."

"I wanted to, but Jack's afraid of you," I said. "Guess what?"

"What?" Craddoc asked, sitting close beside me on the couch.

"I can play pool!"

"Good. Now maybe you can stop sulking in corners when we go to parties."

"I don't sulk in corners!" I gave him a hard shove, which knocked him on the floor where Honey Bear had been sleeping. She skittered away, and I snatched her up and hugged her to me.

"See what you did," Craddoc said, picking himself up. "You almost killed your birthday present."

"Nooo." I petted Honey Bear while the boys discussed whether or not the Fircrest football team would take the state title.

"You going to Seattle on the rooter bus Thursday?" Craddoc asked me.

"I can't. I promised my dad I'd baby-sit for him because it's his wedding anniversary. You coming to my Christmas concert?"

"Well, I don't know about that. . . . Have you done your Christmas shopping?"

"No, not all."

"I don't have any turnouts next week. How about we take a trip to Seattle after school on Monday to Christmas shop? You can help me pick out my mother's present."

I put Honey Bear down on the floor. "Oh, I can't next Monday. I have choir rehearsal."

"You could miss one of those, couldn't you?"

"Could you miss a turnout before a big game?"

101

"Well, that's different. You already know the songs, don't you? Anyway, choir is just like junior varsity. Wait till you make neophonics."

Craddoc doesn't take no easily, part of being an only child, I guess, but I hung in there. "Practicing is how I'll get a chance at neophonics."

"Nooo, you're good enough now."

"I can't let Mr. Krakowski down, Craddoc." My voice was getting screechy.

The muscles in Craddoc's jaw twitched. Jack stood up. "Krakowski would freak if she didn't show up for the dress rehearsal, man. She's got two solos."

After a few seconds Craddoc shrugged, took the pool cue Jack handed him, and played two games before he decided it was about time to take me home. On the way out the door, I flashed a thank-you to Jack and reminded him to bring his essay on Thursday when his suspension was up.

Thursday came, and Jack remembered, and it was a good thing, too. Miss Bickford held his paper in her hand like it was a toad. "This was due Monday."

"I couldn't be here Monday," he explained politely. "Mr. Piker told me to hand in my homework today."

She took in an exasperated breath, thought a minute, and then put his paper in the wire basket on her desk.

Home free, I thought to myself.

Jack and I walked down to the pep assembly together

after class. "I hope you haven't got any firecrackers," I said.

"No. I had a long talk with my folks, and I promised my mom I'd give it a good try."

"What about your dad?"

"He thinks it's up to me. Either I go to school or I go to work."

"Isn't school easier?"

"Maybe easier, if you can stomach it. I worked up in Alaska with my uncle last summer, and I can go back up."

We were nearing the gym and could hear the stomping of feet and the chanting.

"We will win!

"We will win!

"We will win!"

"Do you think we'll win the state play-offs?" I asked Jack as we went through the gym doors.

"If the defense holds and Craddoc gets a chance to boot one."

Up in the bleachers, in the midst of the roar when Leanne Elder introduced the team, I wished I were going to the King Dome to see the game instead of baby-sitting. Except baby-sitting meant I'd have the money for Craddoc's Christmas present.

My dad wasn't home when I arrived at his condominium. Jeanne was dressed and ready to go and sat down and had a talk with me while she waited. "I've been thinking," she started out, "that I could work part-time if I had some help around the house and someone to watch the baby."

You mean someone to *clean* your house and *take care* of the baby, I thought to myself.

"If you'd be interested," she went on, "I'd sure be glad to pay you, and we've got three bedrooms so you could have your own room and your own things just as you do at your mother's place. What do you think about it?"

"I don't know how that would work. Mama has custody of us."

"You're fifteen. If your mother put up a fuss because she didn't want to lose the child support money, you might have to briefly appear in court. It wouldn't be any problem. At your age you get to choose which parent you want to live with. I think we'd be easier to live with than your mother." She ended her speech with a bright smile. I didn't know what she did for part-time work. Sales?

"I'll think about it," I told her. "I probably won't decide until Christmas is over, anyway."

"No rush," she assured me. Dad was coming in the door, and she got up to hug him.

He gave her his briefcase and came over to the davenport to sit beside me. "You get prettier every time I see you."

"Surprised I didn't stay a fat blob?"

"No. No. Most kids grow out of their baby fat."

"I think I had more than baby fat hanging on me."

My dad looks something like Jack Nicholson, but he can't admit to a bald spot, so he parts his hair over one ear and swirls a long brown lock across his blank forehead. He carefully smoothed the lock in place as he thought up his answer. "Well, no matter how fat you were, you still were a lovable little kid."

"That's not how I remember being. Your lady friend found my blubber repulsive enough."

"Oh, well . . . uh . . ."

I watched him fumble that one. The same way he'd fumbled years ago when his lady friend telegraphed a frown to stop him from asking me to go out with them again.

Jeanne returned from stashing the briefcase. "What lady friend was that?"

"Just some broad." Dad got up from the davenport. "Come on. Let's check out the town."

I thought about Jeanne's offer after they left. In either home, I understood clearly, I'd be the Cinderella, but with Jeanne I'd get paid. While I fed and changed the baby, I kept the radio on for news breaks. At ten, when Dad and Jeanne came home, the score at the King Dome was still nothing to nothing.

As soon as I got up in the morning, I headed for the radio in the kitchen. Before I could turn it on, Robyn announced, "Fircrest won."

"How do you know?" I asked her.

"I heard it on the TV news. Seven to ten. Craddoc made another field goal."

"Aw right!"

Mama was sitting at the table drinking coffee. "That Craddoc's quite a boy," she said.

I expected to see Craddoc in the commons when I got to school. None of the football players or cheerleaders were there. Strange. I went up to home ec early and found Diane and Sharon standing around our table. Jenny looked three ways when she saw me.

"What's Craddoc got to say?" Sharon asked me as I sat down.

"About winning? I haven't seen him yet."

"Not about winning. About the bust with Katie Bentler." Sharon's beady eyes were gleaming, and a warning stripe of fear shot across my insides.

"What bust?"

"Katie Bentler, Craddoc, Sue Lyons, and Jamison all went to the game together, and then they partied afterwards, and Mrs. Bentler caught them trying to bring Katie in the house, and she called all the parents and the principal and told them."

"Told them what?"

"That they'd all been *drinking*!" Sharon said it so loud Mrs. Ash looked up from her desk.

"I'd better go or I'll be late." Diane split.

"Diane said there's going to be a hearing this afternoon," Sharon went on. "She said the boys might get their letters pulled and the girls will have to resign."

Mrs. Ash moved to the front of the room. "Please take your seat, Sharon."

I looked at Jenny, and she gave me a weak, sympathetic smile. "Don't believe everything Sharon says," she whispered before Mrs. Ash started roll. "Wait till you talk to Craddoc."

We were back in the main home ec room after the sewing unit was over, and Mrs. Ash spent this hour reviewing Christmas cookie recipes we were going to use in the three school days before winter vacation began. I looked straight at her while she lectured, but none of her words registered in my head.

There had to be some mistake, I kept telling myself. Craddoc didn't drink, and he would have gone on the team bus to Seattle. Maybe Jamison and Craddoc had just bumped into Katie and Sue and offered to take them home, and Sharon, as usual, made a big thing of it. Only, Diane would know what happened, and if Craddoc had wanted to be with Katie, last night would have been the perfect time. Or maybe Katie and Sue had been partying and had asked Craddoc and Jamison for a ride home. If that was right, then Craddoc and Jamison wouldn't be in any trouble.

The minutes dragged on, and Mrs. Ash droned on. My fingers tingled, and when I knew I couldn't stand another second, the bell rang. I rose in my chair instantly. "I'm going to find Jack and see what he knows."

107

Jenny grabbed her books. "I'll go with you."

We caught Jack coming down the hall toward the English room, and I pulled him to a corner away from the traffic. "Jack, what happened last night?"

"I don't know much about it. I saw Craddoc this morning, and all he said was that Bentler was drunk on her butt."

"He must have said more than that," Jenny insisted.

"Well, I don't know any more. Oh, he said Mrs. Bentler lost it and called all the parents and wouldn't let Jamison drive his car home."

"But what about Craddoc?" I said.

"Craddoc's O.K."

"But what did Craddoc do last night?"

Jack turned at the sound of the bell. "Jeez, I can't be late."

We were late. No more than one minute, but Miss Bickford had called the roll and that gave her an excuse.

She placed the green grade book on her desk and took up the stack of dittos. She counted out the number for each row and handed them to the students in the front seats to be passed along. When she came to Jack's row, she paused. "By the way, Jack, I hope you realize that from now on you're in a no-credit situation in this class."

"Because I was one minute late?" Jack asked.

She moved on, counting her dittos, obviously not intending to answer Jack. When every student had a paper, Miss Bickford gave us directions for filling them out. "You

108

have twenty minutes to finish this quiz. Please do so quietly."

The quiz was on the punctuation of subordinate clauses. I finished mine quickly and took it up to her desk. She shook her head in refusal. "I'll collect them all when everyone is finished, Elsie. Please take your seat."

"Miss Bickford, I had a personal problem," I said, leaning toward her. "And I kept Jack out in the hall talking to me after the bell rang."

Miss Bickford raised her eyebrows. "Are you in a no-credit situation, Elsie?"

"I don't think so. I haven't been absent or tardy much."

"Correct. It's only when you've been absent and tardy as much as Jack has that one time makes a difference. Jack may discuss this with his counselor or Mr. Piker, but I'm not going to discuss it further."

Jack joined us at her desk. "May I go now to see the counselor?"

She nodded. "Certainly.

"And, Jack," she called after him, "I think you'd be better off dropping the class and taking a study hall instead of sitting in here."

I returned to my seat. Poor Jack. I was a big help. Miss Bickford collected the quizzes, and I went over it all once more. Jack hadn't said Craddoc was in trouble, so maybe Craddoc . . .

The principal's voice came over the P.A. with the morning announcements. The drama club would meet after school in the little theater, there would be a brief faculty meeting before school Monday, the Christmas concert would be held next Tuesday evening . . . "and it is with great pride that I congratulate the members of the football team and the coaches for bringing home the state trophy. I personally would have been satisfied with their winning the WESCO conference and the Northwest district play-offs, but they hung in there to go all the way, and I know all of you are as proud of them as I am.

"Now, many of you are aware"—the principal's voice took on a sober tone, and panic clutched my stomach— "that some football players and cheerleaders chose not to represent our school in a dignified manner last night. But a few individuals, failing us and themselves, should not detract from the character and victory of the majority participating in the event.

"This concludes the announcements."

Wet Sand

I didn't go to chorus, even though we were rehearsing for the concert. I didn't go to geometry, either. I sat in the far corner of the commons, eating corn chips and staring at the wall. I hate corn chips, but the other things in the vending machines taste worse.

First lunch came and went. Craddoc had first lunch. Not that it made any difference. It was after fifth period when he slid onto the bench beside me. I didn't look up.

"Somebody said you were sitting in here," he said.

"I thought you had a meeting this afternoon."

"Not till two o'clock. So you heard, huh?"

"It would be pretty hard not to."

"What are you burned up about?" There was a warning sharpness in his voice that I ignored.

"Oh, little details like your asking me if *I* was going to take the *rooter bus*, then taking Katie Bentler in the car."

"It was Jamison's car."

"What happened to the team bus?"

"The team bus went. We got permission to go ahead and check out the place."

"How convenient."

"When I found you at Jack's, I didn't assume anything was wrong," he said slowly.

"Of course not. I was helping him with his English, not getting drunk with him." It was too much. I hadn't meant to say that much.

He got up and stood in front of me. "It would have been nice, Elsie, if for once you could have been on my side instead of always assuming I'm some kind of butt."

I watched him leave the commons and wished I'd told him that I'd been baby-sitting for his Christmas present while he was partying with Bentler. If we ever got back together, he could tell me *he* was sorry, and I'd be the one to give a little speech about being worthy of trust.

The bell for sixth period rang. School felt like a bunch of junk, so I gathered up my books and went home on the Metro. When Robyn came in, I was finishing off a box of cookies and a bottle of Coke.

"Why are you home so early?" she asked.

"What do you care?"

"Sorry!" She picked up the cookie box and shook it.

"Giving up your anorexia nervosa?"

I snatched the box back from her. "Get your own food."

"Forget it. I'm going over to Cecile's."

I put my empty glass down on the kitchen table as another wave of depression went over me. The worst part of the mess was Jenny's birthday party being the next day. How was I going to get through that? Or the night, for that matter.

I didn't fall asleep until after the clock bonged three, and then I had a strange dream. I dreamed I was at a shopping center, weaving in and out of the crowd, when I saw Craddoc ahead of me. He had a girl with him. It was raining, and she was wearing a plastic cape with a rain hood. I followed them, trying to get closer and closer to see who she was.

They stopped in the entrance of a department store. Craddoc leaned down and kissed the girl good-bye on her forehead and strode away. I wiggled through the crowd as fast as I could to catch her in the store before she disappeared. I spotted the wet black cape at a jewelry counter and went around to the other side of the counter where I could look back at her face. It wasn't a girl at all. It was Craddoc's mother.

At ten-thirty I dragged myself out of bed, yanked the covers over my wet pillow, and plodded into the bathroom to stare at my ugly reflection in the mirror. I'd promised Jenny I'd be at her house right after lunch to help her with the decorations. Robyn was going to clean

Wet Sand

our house first if I had to break every bone in her body to make her do it. I couldn't even stand to look at the place.

When I got to Jenny's, Sharon and Diane were sitting at the dining room table with her, stringing our baked Christmas ornaments on tree holders. I laid my jacket over a chair before I sat down. "What's been happening?"

"I made candy," Jenny said, passing me the dish. "Have some."

Sharon leaned over my shoulder to choose the fattest piece. "Jenny, will your parents be home tonight? I hardly ever see them."

"Me neither," Jenny said. "I think they're competing on who can do the most overtime."

Diane thoughtfully licked her fingers. "Did you ever think that your mom might be under-mated?"

This was better than fudge to Sharon. She plunked herself back in her seat. "My mother says . . ."

"Forget it," Diane told her. "Nobody wants to hear what your mother says."

The muscles in Sharon's face clenched as she forced her concentration on tying a Christmas ornament. Diane put up with her only at parties because of Jenny, and Sharon couldn't afford to blow that. If Sharon's and Jenny's families weren't old friends, Sharon wouldn't have a chance around Diane and she knew it.

I took the opportunity of the silence to casually ask again, "Well, what's been happening over the principal's meeting?"

114

"Sue and Katie resigned," Diane said, "and Jamison's getting his letter yanked."

"What about Craddoc?"

Diane dangled an ornament in the air to imagine how it would look hanging on the tree. "Oh, nothing about him. He never drinks."

"You said *all* of them were drinking."

"Not me." Diane put the ornament in the pile with the others. "That was Sharon."

Sharon shrugged away the blame. "Well, I didn't know."

"Shee-it!"

"Don't cry, Elsie." Jenny came over to my chair and put her arm around me. "Don't cry. Craddoc will understand."

"No, he won't. Not this time. I believed that lying Sharon and accused him of getting drunk with Katie Bentler."

"Don't blame me for your troubles," Sharon said. "I only told you what I heard."

Jenny got me a tissue, and I blew my nose. And then the tears started over again. I rose shakily from my chair. "I better go home."

Jenny kept her arm around me. "Do you want me to go with you?"

"No, you stay and get ready for your party."

She took me to the door and gave me an extra hug good-bye. "When Craddoc comes to pick you up tonight, just explain to him you got the wrong story."

"I won't get the chance. He'll never show."

I was right. I got dressed for the party, anyway, on the faint hope he would come. At nine-forty I called his house.

"Craddoc isn't here, Elsie," his mother told me.

"Do you know where he is?"

"No, I'm sorry. I *do not*." Her tone meant "and get lost" as clearly as if she'd said it.

"Thank you," I managed. "Good-bye."

I paced the empty living room, trying to lose Mrs. Shaw's sting and wiping under my eyes so my makeup wouldn't smear. I *had* to go to Jenny's party. Or at least show. Mama and Robyn were at a movie, so I locked the front door behind me and started out in the dark.

Christmas lights were twinkling around the eaves of Jenny's house, a blast of music hit the street each time her door was opened, and I could see dancing kids through the windows, but I couldn't make myself cross the street and go up her steps. I headed down the road toward Edmonds beach. Craddoc's leaving me was burning into my head. I had turned on him when his friends were in trouble, so why should he show up? To get accused again of doing things he never did? I was just like my mother.

My heels sank into the sand when I left the concrete. The moon flickering on the sound made the water look like someone had thrown a broken mirror across its surface. If I followed the path, swimming out and out until I was too tired to swim any more, that would be all there was to it. Easy.

116

Headlights on the road startled me. I turned, and a flashlight beam from the car struck my face.

"What are you doing out here, lonely little girl?"

The emptiness of the beach swept over me.

"How about getting in the nice, warm car, lonely little girl?"

A latch clicked. Oh, God, let somebody come.

"Maybe you need me to take you in."

I stepped back into the shallow water. Two more headlights coming slowly. Please stop and help. Please stop and help. Please.

The second car drew up behind the first. The moon shone on the colored bar across the top and I let my breath out. Oh, thank you.

The car door opened, and a tall policeman got out. "Some problem here?"

"No, no, officer," a voice called from the first car. "Just pulled up to see if this little girl was in trouble."

The car slid off into the night as the policeman walked over to me. "A bit late for you to be out, isn't it?"

You Just Lost a Daughter

"I don't know what her problem is or what your family problems are." The policeman kept a grip on my arm as he talked to Mama in the doorway. "But most people are aware that if a young girl is allowed to wander the streets after dark, she's inviting trouble."

Mama's eyes narrowed the way they do when she's angry. "She wasn't supposed to be wandering the streets. She was supposed to be at the Sawyers' house for a birthday party. I have *always* confirmed every place she goes."

"I'll leave her in your care then, and I won't expect to be picking her up again tonight." The policeman let go of my arm and walked off to his patrol car.

Mama looked down at me as I stood shivering on the porch. "Proudest moment of my life."

"Mine, too," I murmured.

She jerked her head toward the lighted living room. "Get in the house!"

Robyn was sitting in a chair, watching us with round eyes. She still had her coat on, so they must have just gotten home from the movie. Mama faced me, putting her hands on her hips. "All right. Let's have your story."

"I—I went to Jenny's house like I told you I was going to do. Only I didn't go in. I went for a walk instead. I was upset because I had a fight with Craddoc yesterday."

"That makes sense. You had a fight with Craddoc yesterday so you didn't go into Jenny's house tonight. Why didn't you stay home?"

"Because I thought Jenny would expect me on her birthday."

"Oh." Mama nodded. "That's why you went to the beach. Well, since you don't have a boyfriend any more, you won't mind staying in the house after dark until you're old enough to be trusted out."

"Except," I said hurriedly, remembering the Christmas concert, "for Tuesday night. I have to . . ."

"I don't care what you 'have to.' I'm not opening my door to be greeted by the police again. You're not getting out for a long, long time. Understand?"

"Mama, wait a minute." I concentrated on the picture behind her to avoid the blast of fury. "Wait a minute. I didn't do anything wrong, and this is a school function which I have to . . ."

She snatched my shoulder with a clawed hand, forcing me to look at her. "*You* wait a minute. I told you *not* to tell me what you have to do."

"But it isn't fair. I'll go live with Dad if . . ."

A stinging slap knocked my head to the side. "Don't you ever threaten me with your father."

I straightened up from the blow, said clearly, "You just lost a daughter," turned from her, and went to my bedroom.

I paced until I cooled enough to make decisions. Maybe I couldn't have Craddoc back, maybe I'd screwed up too badly this time. But I could get the rest of my life together—starting with her. If I lived with her or didn't, she was never going to be Mama to me again. She had never been a mama, she wasn't interested in being a mama, and the sooner I knocked off that baby talk the better off I'd be.

That night would be the end of Cinderella, too. From then on I'd do one-third of the work when she was home and one-half the work when she wasn't. And if she didn't like that, I'd be a wage earner at Dad's. And no more little cowed thing, taking any punishment she wanted to give me for any imaginary evil. I was going to sing my solos in the Christmas concert, and she didn't need to come, since she never had, but she couldn't stop me either.

120

Bitterness oozed from me as I imagined another confrontation over my leaving for the concert and her screaming about restrictions and me packing my things and calling Dad to pick me up.

Robyn stuck her head in the middle of that fantasy after she inched my door open. "Can I come in?"

"It looks like you already are."

She sat on the edge of my bed in her pajamas. I've never seen her so solemn. "Elsie, don't move out. Please don't."

"What possible difference could it make to you?"

"It would be so lonely here without you."

"You mean you might have to clean up your own messes."

She bit on her fingernail awhile. "I guess I always figured you could take care of everything."

"Cinderella?"

"No, my big sister." She slid off the bed. "If you stay, I promise there'll be some changes around here."

"You're right about that," I said, and went back to my decisions as she went out the door.

I got pen and paper from my desk and brought them to my bed. With Honey Bear in my lap, I wrote until I got to decision number 4: *I will try to be nice to everyone, but when someone causes trouble like Sharon, I will ignore them.*

That brought Craddoc close, and I put down the pen and watched my tears drop into Honey Bear's fur. She licked my hands in sympathy, and I hugged her and told her how much I wished she could give me *him* for Christmas.

Mother came in to see me before she left for work the next morning. "Elsie, I wanted to tell you," she started off, "that I didn't intend to slap you. What you said about your father upset me."

I watched her from my pillow. "When you're fifteen years old, you are allowed to live with the parent of your choice."

That pissed her, but she kept her cool. "You know, your father did a good job of making my life miserable."

That's no excuse for making mine miserable, I thought, but I let her go on.

"I've been under a lot of stress lately. Real estate isn't moving very well, and I've been worried about the house payments, and I want you girls to turn out right. When I saw you with the police, I thought you'd done something terrible. And I just overreacted." She waited for me to say something, and I didn't. I didn't tell her how pleased I was that she had so much trust in me.

She ran her hand through her hair. "Robyn needs you, too, you realize."

"What for? When I was her age, I was a full-time baby-sitter."

"Yes, well, I know I've had to give you a lot of respon-sibility." She looked nervously at her watch. "I'm late for an appointment with some buyers. Uh . . . forget about

122

the restrictions, O.K.?" She hesitated a bit longer, then left.

Robyn brought me breakfast in bed, which was pretty nice of her. It was grapefruit, toast and jam, and tea. "I knew you wouldn't feel like eggs," she explained. She was right again.

She let Honey Bear out and came back and watched me eat until she had the nerve to ask, "What happened between you and Craddoc?"

I tried to explain about the fight, but she couldn't get it.

"I don't see why you believed Sharon. She's such a wimp."

"It wasn't only Sharon. The principal said football players and cheerleaders." I guess I sounded irritated, because she took the tray and split.

I managed to get up to make dinner. Mother came home just as Robyn and I were finished eating. She sat down at the table, and I did not serve her. Instead, I said to Robyn, "I got dinner. You can do the dishes."

Mother looked at me. "It wouldn't hurt to help, would it?"

"Why? When I was her age, I made the dinner and did the dishes both."

"That's O.K. That's O.K.," Robyn put in before Mother could reply. "I don't mind doing them."

I left the kitchen and went to my bedroom to work on my studies. "You spacin' out?" I'd hear Craddoc say in my

123

head when I'd stop for a minute and stare out of my window while waves of sadness rode over me.

I saw Craddoc Tuesday morning in the commons. He nodded to me as I walked by. I nodded back like we were distant cousins. When I was out of his sight, I slipped into the girls' lavatory to steady myself. Katie Bentler was in there, combing her hair. She didn't look like much out of her cheerleader's uniform. Pasty face with a little pig's nose and baggy pants and clunky shoes. I went into a stall so I wouldn't have to talk to her. How could I have been so dumb as to think Craddoc would want her?

Sliced Tomato Eyes

Jenny called before dinner and said her family wanted to hear me in the concert, and why didn't I bring Robyn and we'd all drive together in their van. Robyn and I arrived a little early at the Sawyers', which was fine with Kenny because he wanted to show off his rats to Robyn. I found Mrs. Sawyer and Jenny in the kitchen wrapping pieces of chicken in foil.

"Elsie," Mrs. Sawyer said, "I hear you're a single woman again."

"Yes," I agreed. "I did myself in."

She laughed. "Everybody does themselves in. You're just more honest than most to admit it." She stacked the wrapped chicken and lifted the package over to the freezer,

125

while Jenny held the door open for her.

"What I can't figure out," Jenny said, "is what's in those little boxes in there."

Mrs. Sawyer put the chicken on the shelf and took out three small boxes. "These? I can throw these away now that they're frozen. They're my population control."

"Your what?"

Mrs. Sawyer dumped the boxes into the garbage pail. "My population control."

"Ohh." I finally got it. "That's why Kenny was having trouble with his baby rat count."

"Mo-ther!"

"Well"—she scooped the chicken scraps into a paper towel and threw them in the garbage, too—"what did you want me to do? Flush them down the toilet? This way they just shiver a little and go to sleep."

Jenny shook her head. "You're unreal."

Jack arrived about that time, and Jenny got her fox-collar jacket and met him in the living room. He looked her over with a frown. "What happened to your own jacket?"

"This is mine," Jenny said.

"It looks like something my mother'd wear," he told her.

I glanced at Mrs. Sawyer as we went out the door to see if there was pleased revenge on her face. There wasn't. That lady must really have it together.

A concert is one place I'm not shy. As the choir marched

126

up to the stage, I gave the audience a big smile. There was a moment when I thought I saw Craddoc in the back of the little theater, but when the lights went up, he was not there.

Getting in the van to go home, Kenny insisted on sitting next to me. I was the "star," he said. Mr. and Mrs Sawyer agreed, and Jenny bet I'd be greater than the Go-Go's someday. Robyn didn't say much until Mr. Sawyer had the van pulled out of the school parking lot. "I saw somebody who looked like Craddoc."

"Shaw?" Jack said. "He came in to hear Elsie sing. What did you expect?"

"Why didn't he go with us?" Kenny asked.

"You'll find out someday," Jack said, "when some woman puts you down the way Elsie put him down."

"She puts herself down worse," Mrs. Sawyer said.

"That may be," Jack admitted, "but it doesn't make it easier on a guy."

"You know, Elsie"—Mrs. Sawyer turned around to face us—"you deserve to be happy."

"Oh, oh," Jenny said, "here we go. Now, Elsie, every night you can write seventy times that you deserve to be happy. Then you can write seventy times seven that you deserve love. Mom's got all the magic. And if that doesn't work, she'll boil up a few herbs for you. . . . Oh, wait a minute, wait a minute. First you've got to forgive yourself for having been fat and learn to love yourself. *And then* you write down seven times seventy . . ."

"Jenny, you aren't funny. Elsie does deserve love." Mrs. Sawyer turned around to face the front of the car.

Jack reached out and put his hand on my shoulder. "You deserve it, foxy lady, but Craddoc deserved a few things, too."

You will *not* cry, I told myself. You absolutely will not cry. You little baby, you will *not* cry.

I could feel Robyn watching me in the dark, and suddenly she said in a loud voice, "This big van is really nice for a family. I wish we had a car that could take at least three."

"It is nice"—Mrs. Sawyer nodded—"and it would be even nicer to have a big house."

Mr. Sawyer let out a groan.

"Now you can't say," she said to him, "that it wouldn't be nice for the children to at least have a rec room."

"How many six-day work weeks do you figure it will take you before you have the down payment?" he asked her.

"I haven't got it *exactly* figured out. . . ."

"You'll get it figured out, I have no doubt." He turned the car into our driveway and, before he got out of his door to help us, he patted his wife's head. "I think I'll burn your copies of *Ms.*"

When we were in our house, Robyn took her coat off and flung it on a chair. "That's the neatest family."

"They have their troubles just like everybody else, and

if you leave your coat there, *you're* picking it up eventually. I'm not."

"You don't get to have the glass slipper from the prince, then." She picked up her coat and held it under her chin. "Maybe you ought to buy a Christmas card and draw tears on it and send it to Craddoc."

"Real subtle."

Mother came in, looked at our coats, and asked where we'd been.

"To Elsie's Christmas concert," Robyn said. "She was the star. You should have been there."

"No one even told me about it."

As I left for my room, I could hear Mother's complaining voice behind me and Robyn's reply, "What did you expect? All you ever do is rag at her."

In the morning I stood outside the study hall before second period instead of going to my English class. I figured the counselor system would work at least one time for me. Jack came along just as the bell rang and told me to wait a minute until he got a library pass.

We walked together to the library, with Jack mumbling an X-rated description of his shop teacher. "Do you know how he called the roll this morning?" he asked me when we were seated behind the bookshelves.

"No, how?"

"Like this: 'Cameron? Sliced tomato eyes. Earl? Sliced tomato eyes. Jack? Oh, you haven't got sliced tomato eyes today.' Do you know what he asked me Monday?"

"No, what?"

"He asked me why I didn't quit and go to the cracker box down the hill."

"Cracker box?"

"The alternative school."

"Oh."

"My mom says the central school administration has appointed a study group to find out why kids drop out of school. Unreal, huh?"

I admitted it was, and Jack seemed wound down enough then to answer my questions. "Does Craddoc have another girl yet?"

He slumped his head into his hand in complete disgust. "Oh, Elsie, don't start that again."

"No, wait a minute, Jack. You don't understand. What I mean is do you think it would work if I apologized?"

"It's possible but not probable. How many times have you said you're sorry?"

"Twice before."

"Well? Craddoc's not an idiot, you know." He must have seen something in my face because he sat up straight and smiled. "But . . . what have you got to lose? Go for it!"

I wanted to pry some more reassurances out of Jack, but I knew that would irritate him, so I went on down to the counselor's office and asked her about neophonics, which I already knew all about, but which she didn't know I already knew all about.

130

The Letter

Thursday was the first day of winter vacation. I'd planned to finish my Christmas shopping, but Jeanne called in the morning to ask if I'd baby-sit for a few hours, and more money sounded good. I told her I'd be over after I showered and had breakfast.

Mother came into the bathroom while I was blow-drying my hair. She had that pinched look she gets when something's bugging her. "Somebody tipped over my nail polish in the cabinet and polish is on the shelf."

"I wouldn't know anything about it. I wasn't the one who did the bathrooms last Saturday, and I don't use nail polish." I fluffed my hair with the dryer and waited for her anger to turn my stomach.

"Somebody spilled that bottle, and it's going to get cleaned up."

I shrugged, keeping my eyes on the mirror as I concentrated on the middle of my body. Nothing. I didn't care if she was pissed or not. I yanked the dryer cord out of the wall and left her standing in the bathroom, stuck with her discontent.

Jeanne greeted me at the door with the baby in her arms. "He's got a cold and screams every time I put him down. I'm exhausted from holding him."

I looked over her messy living room as I shed my coat and took the baby. "If you want me to straighten this up while you're gone, you'll have to pay me extra."

"Gladly," she said, and got ready to leave.

She gave me a ten-dollar "Christmas bonus" when she returned and asked me if I had thought any more about moving in with them.

"I'll probably stay with Mother and Robyn for now," I said, "but give me a call when you need me."

"Nuts." She plunked herself down on the davenport. "I get cabin fever staying in here all day."

I took the Metro to Aurora Village to hunt for Grandma's, Mother's, and Jenny's presents. And Craddoc's, just in case. I finished faster than I'd thought I would and was wandering through the pet shop in Woolworth's, looking for a Christmas bone for Honey Bear, when I spotted the dog collars. Perfect! I could send one to Craddoc, saying I'd wear it until he got me trained. Maybe that would do it.

132

A woman in a black suit came down the aisle as I was adjusting a red collar on my neck. "What are you doing, you idiot!" she snapped. "Trying out for an apprenticeship with Phyllis Schlafly?"

I took the collar off, with a big red face, and went home. Robyn had our tiny Christmas tree on the coffee table and was arranging presents under it. "I'll wrap yours if you want," she offered.

"Great." I gave her my packages and headed for my room to try a letter to Craddoc.

Dear Craddoc,

I wouldn't write you this letter—I'd leave you alone because you're probably better off without me—except I can't stop hurting. If I feel better a little while, I finger the misery and it's still there. Nothing makes it go away.

In the night I think about Jamison being your best friend and how I'd feel if you shut me down when Jenny was in trouble, and I hate myself so much I can't stand it. I wake Honey Bear up and hug her and she licks me, trying to show me she understands and loves me, which makes me cry more.

I'm trying to cut the bad things out of me, Craddoc. I'm not afraid of my mother any more. I don't call her Mama, and I stopped being Cinderella. I can't promise I'll *never* be jealous again. When I think of Katie Bentler in her cat costume pawing you and licking your face, I get sick to my stomach. And I saw her the other day, and she isn't even pretty.

Jack tried to tell me you'd never like her. He says I'm jealous because I want to keep you in a box when I'm not playing with you. I don't think that's my problem. Since I haven't been sleeping nights, I've had a lot of time to go over my problem. I think I see things wrong. I'm positive I'm seeing them right at the time, but it turns out wrong. I think fear does it to me. Like wearing green-colored glasses or having kaleidoscopes for eyes. You see it one way. Change your head. And see it another way.

I dreamed I saw you with another girl, and I followed you to see who she was, and it turned out to be your mother. That's how dumb I am. In the beginning of the dream I was sure you were with another girl.

Please don't give up on me, Craddoc. Fifteen isn't too old to change. I'm not afraid of my mother any more, and I've been afraid of her since I was a little kid. That's a start, right?

My mother says being sorry doesn't help. I'm sorry anyway, Craddoc. Real, real sorry.

I hope you have a Merry Christmas.

Love,
Elsie

I read the letter over. Before I could lose my nerve, I sealed it in an envelope, took my last bill out of my purse, and went out to ask Robyn if she'd like to make a dollar.

"Doing what?" she said.

"Delivering this letter for me."

"Where?"

"To Craddoc's mailbox. Otherwise, it won't get there before Christmas."

She smiled. "Maybe I'll read it on the way."

"No, Robyn. Come on."

She put her colored ribbons down and snatched the letter from me. "You can keep your money."

The morning of Christmas Eve came, and there was no call or visit or note from Craddoc, no present from him under the tree. I waited all day, hoping, with my heart racing each time the phone rang. By nighttime I was so down I had to dig my fingernails into my palms to keep from crying.

We had Grandma over for dinner. She picked on Mother the way Mother picks on me. I couldn't see why Mother didn't tell her to back off.

My presents were O.K. I got a typewriter and typing lessons from Mother, a dog brush for Honey Bear from Robyn, and a check from Grandma. Grandma didn't like any of her presents. The slip Mother gave her she didn't need. She already had three in her dresser drawer. Perfume started up her hay fever, and the earrings were pretty, but they emphasized her wrinkled neck. Robyn and I were glad when Mother took her home.

"I hope I never get that old," Robyn said, gathering up

135

the tissue paper and throwing it in the fireplace.

I got out the vacuum. "Are you sure you left my letter to Craddoc in the right mailbox?"

"I didn't put it in his mailbox. I gave it to him."

"How come?" I turned off the vacuum to hear her answer.

"Because I wanted to be sure he got it. I rang his doorbell, and he came to the door."

"What did he say?"

"Thanks."

When we finished cleaning the living room, my present for Craddoc sat by itself under the tree. I left it there, pottied Honey Bear, and went to bed to stare up in the dark at the ceiling until the clock bonged three, my magic hour.

"Get up, Elsie! Get up, Elsie, Santa Claus is here."

"Robyn!" I shrugged away from her.

"Get up, Elsie. It's Christmas and Santa Claus is here!"

I focused my eyes on my window. It was pitch-black outside. I peered at my clock. Six o'clock. "Robyn, you're crazy!"

She yanked my covers off and dragged at my body. "Quick. Get up and wash your teeth."

"My teeth?"

"Yes, come on." She pulled and pushed me into the bathroom, smeared toothpaste on my brush, and handed it to me. Sleepily I brushed my teeth, let her lead me into the den, and watched her dash from the room.

She was back in a second with a man wearing a Santa Claus mask. What??

"Craddoc!!" I screamed.

"Sh! Sh!" Robyn whispered. "You'll wake Mama."

"Oh, Craddoc!" I reached out to hug him and then burst into laughter.

Robyn was halfway out the door and turned around, puzzled. Craddoc took off his mask. "What's funny?"

"Oh, Craddoc!" I put my arms around him and kissed him. "I couldn't figure out why Robyn was making me brush my teeth."

"I thought it would be nicer," Robyn said defensively.

I swung back away from Craddoc with my arms still around his neck. "It is, Robyn. It is. And you're the neatest sister in the whole world."

"Well. Merry Christmas, you two." And she went out, closing the door behind her, while Craddoc pulled me close for another Christmas kiss.

ABOUT THE AUTHOR

Barthe DeClements is a school counselor in Edmonds, Washington. She has also worked as a psychologist and teacher. About her first book, *Nothing's Fair in Fifth Grade* (Viking), *Parents' Choice* said, "With compassion and humor, Barthe DeClements has written an absolutely marvelous first novel." *School Library Journal:* "Characters are drawn lovingly and respectfully. . . . The book is fun and worthwhile to read."

Barthe DeClements says, "I thrive on space and solitude. Whenever I have them, I write." She lives in a log house, built by the youngest of her four children, on the Pilchuck River near Snohomish, Washington.